★THE BOXER★

BY KATHLEEN KARR

It Ain't Always Easy

Oh, Those Harper Girls!

Gideon and the Mummy Professor

The Cave

In the Kaiser's Clutch

The Great Turkey Walk

Man of the Family

The Boxer

★ THE ★

BOXER

KATHLEEN

KARR

FARRAR STRAUS GIROUX

━ NEW YORK ━

With thanks to Tom Quinn, historian of the New York Athletic Club

Library of Congress Cataloging-in-Publication Data
Karr, Kathleen.
　The boxer / Kathleen Karr.
　　p.　cm.
　Summary: Having learned how to box while in prison, fifteen-year-old Johnny sets out to discover if he can make a decent living as a fighter in late nineteenth-century New York City.
　ISBN 0-374-30921-3
　[1. Boxing—Fiction.　2. Prisons—Fiction.　3. Prisoners—Fiction.　4. New York (N.Y.)—Fiction.]　I. Title.
PZ7.K149 Bo　　2000
[Fic]—dc21　　　　　　　　　　　　　　　　　　99-54794

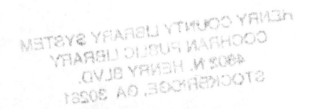

For Mr. Jim Finley,
who welcomed me to his boxing club

For Lance Day,
my expert and patient trainer

And in memory of Jim Jacobs,
who introduced me to the "Sweet Science"

★THE BOXER★

★ ONE ★

State yer name."

"Jo—Johnny."

"Yer proper name."

The shivering was still with me. Couldn't make it stop. Maybe it was my clothes. Sopping wet they were from being dragged through the cold sleet of the midnight streets, and me inside of them. More like it was thoughts of my ma waiting for me back at the tenement that brought on the shakes.

"I ain't got all year! You're holding up the line!"

I was, too. A ragged string of night people shuffled behind me, the likes of which would give Ma heart failure. I finally spit it out. "Woods. John Aloysius Xavier Woods."

A snort. "Your ma sure wasted a lot of saints on you."

The insult didn't even get a rise out of me, the way it usually would. I was in that much trouble, and as wretched as I'd ever been. I just watched the copper write my name in a big ledger.

"State yer age."

"Fifteen. Just."

That made him tip his cap back over his head and give me a look. "*Just* too bad, then. Judge won't be sentencing you as a minor."

Fresh tremors hit me, worse than the last lot.

"Address?"

When he was done with all that, another copper yanked me by the collar and hauled me through the station house. With a *creak* and a *clank* and a shove to the back I found myself in my new lodgings. A jail cell.

But I didn't have the time to take it in. That shove propelled me straight into the closest cot. It wasn't empty, more's the pity. With a curse, its owner tossed me across the room to another cot. For a few minutes I thought I'd been changed into a ball, I was bounced around so fierce. I finally ended up on a second-tier bunk and curled into myself to be good and miserable.

Brought it on my own head, I had. My ma's always been after me not to fight. But what's a little fellow like me meant to do? Seems like there's always been someone after me for one thing or the other, always been someone bigger. Tonight had just seemed like a reasonable solution to a lot of things. Tonight in the room behind Brodie's Saloon. Just my luck Brodie was behind on his payoffs. Just my luck New York City's finest picked tonight for a raid. I twisted up a little tighter, trying not to let too much of me touch the filthy mattress. The bruises from Brodie's back room began to throb. Everywhere, it felt like. I closed my eyes and tried not to breathe the cell's loathsome air.

Where had I gone wrong?

It was already dark when I'd been let out of the sweatshop for the night. No surprise for seven o'clock of a February evening. I pulled my collar up against the hard rain and jammed my hands into my pockets. They stung as usual. When you're doing the finish ironing on men's ready-made shirts all day, your mind had to wander a bit. Then you found your fingers scorched. Better than ruining a shirt, though. They'd take that out of your wages. They took everything out of your wages.

I was turning in the direction of home, thinking about Ma's hot supper that would be waiting for me, thinking about how all five of the little ones would be waiting for me, too. Always treated me like some kind of a hero, they did, each and every night I made it home from work. That made the twelve hours shut up in the Ludlow Street sweater's a little easier. Made it easier turning my wages over to Ma, too. All but a dime a week. My fingers felt for the nickel that was left of last week's pay. There it was, deep down in my trousers pocket. Wouldn't it be nice to have a little more left over each week? Something for a hunk of meat for the potato and cabbage stew after the rent was paid.

That's what I was thinking as I passed Brodie's Saloon. The regular sign was up:

```
┌────────────────────────────────────────────────┐
│              SPARRING TONIGHT!                  │
│      BAREFISTED BATTLES AT THEIR BEST!          │
│       $5 PURSE TO 4-ROUND WINNER!               │
│           LIKELY LADS INVITED                   │
└────────────────────────────────────────────────┘
```

I'd read that sign a hundred times. This time I stopped and read it again. Sure, I was small. But I was fast. Everybody said I was fast. Maybe I could hold up for four rounds. Give just enough back to the other fellow . . . Five dollars was more than I made in two weeks. With five dollars I could get a pair of boots without slapping soles that let in the weather. I could buy Ma a new dress so she wouldn't be ashamed to show her face at mass. I could bring home some extra food— more than just a hunk of meat—to keep that hungry look out of the kids' faces for a few days . . . There were too many things I could do with five dollars. Wasn't even worth continuing the list. Before I could change my mind, I pushed through the door into Brodie's Saloon.

The fug inside almost stopped me cold. I made out the long bar propped up by dozens of men, smoking and raising their pints. Took a step, and almost slid on the rain- and spit-wet sawdust floor. Finally managed to stiffen my shoulders and walk over to the bar.

"Where's Brodie?" I shouted manfully above the din.

I guess it wasn't manfully enough, 'cause no one paid me any mind. I took a deep breath and tried again.

"Where's Brodie?" I bellowed.

The barkeep spotted me and slid closer. "What you want with him, squirt?"

"I'm a likely lad. I'm volunteering."

"For the fights?" He let out a roar.

"Hey!" I could feel my dander rising, like the hair on my head. I pressed closer, waving a fist. "You think I can't do it? You calling John Aloysius Xavier Woods a coward?"

He roared again. "With red hair and a name like that, never. No. I'm calling you a kid."

My fist came closer to his jutting chin. "Call me that after you see me fight."

"All right, all right." He backed off with a grin. "Through the door at the end of the bar. Go sell yourself to Brodie if you can."

"That's more like it." I squared my shoulders again and sauntered in that direction, like I was on top of the world. Like I knew exactly what I was doing. Like Pa used to do before he stopped being on top of the world and just took off on us two years back. And there was the door. I gave it a good shove and swaggered through. Then I blinked.

I'd never been back here before. The room was bigger than the saloon out front, way bigger. Brodie had cobbled together rows of seats out of bare boards, all stepped around a center pit. Those boards were all filled now with frenzied, shouting men. I shoved through part of the crowd to see what they were all so worked up about. Almost swallowed my tongue. There were *rats* down there. Rats. And they were tearing into each other something ferocious. Had dabs of paint on their fur for to tell them apart, I guessed, and the men were shouting:

"Blue! Go, Blue!"

"Green! Come on, Green!"

Well, it was hard to see Blue for all the blood dripping over him. First time I ever felt sorry for a rat. Pretty soon I didn't have to feel sorry anymore. Blue was flat on his back, paws up in the air and stiffening fast. Green sat back on his haunches, twitching his nose nervously.

There was some money changed hands, Green got caught and shoved into a cage, then Brodie himself stepped into the pit.

"Don't go running off, gentlemen," he shouted, " 'cause the main event ain't even close to starting. First we got a few good cockfights coming up, then we'll bring on what you're waiting for." He paused and gave a great wink. "At least what you're waiting for right now. Lovely Lucy and Delicious Delilah won't top off the night with their Fair Fists of Fury till last on the bill."

I pushed through, right into the pit. Brodie finally noticed me.

"Out of the pit, kid. We got business going on here."

I stood my ground. "I've come to fight."

"*You?*"

I took a stance. "Yeah, *me.*"

He let out a roar of laughter better than his bartender's. Then he sobered. "Well, then, and why not? John L. Sullivan had to start somewhere." He jerked his thumb. "Back there, kid. Through the last door. Just wait with the others."

Through the last door I waited and watched. The other fellows hanging around were big. They were stripped down to the waist, and spent a lot of time doing exercises that I'd never seen before. I wondered if I should be stripping down, too, or at least limbering up a little. But it was cold in the back room, so I just stood there with my coat buttoned to the neck. Until Brodie stuck his head in.

"You." He pointed a fat cigar at one of the fellows. "And you." Another. "You're on." His cigar stopped in my direction. "You. Strip down. You get to take on the winner next."

I peeled off layers down to my trousers, then snapped the braces of my suspenders back over my bare shoulders. There wasn't much else to do but listen to the roars of bloodlust coming from the big room behind. They ebbed and flowed, then built into a crescendo. The noise had barely died down when one of those fellows staggered back into the room, swiping at blood dripping from his nose.

"Did you win?" I asked hopefully.

"Yeah. Won a broken nose." He made it to his pile of clothes and started pulling on his shirt. The effort looked painful. "Better get out there," he mumbled, shirt half over his head. "Brodie's waiting. So's Killer Cohen."

"Killer Cohen?"

"Brodie's house fighter. We're just fodder for his fists."

I'd made it as far as the door, but hadn't gotten around to opening it yet. Wasn't sure I wanted to. Another of life's little certainties was beginning to dawn on me. "Any likely lad ever win Brodie's five dollars?"

"Not recent."

Then the door opened for me, and Brodie dragged me straight into the pit. Couldn't call the same place that had rat and cockfights a *ring* any way you looked at it, even if someone had strung up rope in a tight square. Next I was shoved under the rope and Brodie was yelling again.

"In that corner we got the Killer, as per usual. And here, fresh in his braces for his maiden fight, we got"—Brodie stopped long enough to give me another glance—"the Kid! Place your bets, gentlemen, and let the fight begin!"

There I stood in the center of the pit, waiting for a bell. I'd heard somewhere that bouts had taken to using bells to mark off the rounds. I'd also heard that boxers touched fists before starting in. So I waited in the center of the roped-off square for the bell and the shake. Even stretched out my hand, friendly like, when Killer Cohen headed toward me. He grabbed my offered hand with one of his and twisted it behind my back. Sort of woke me up good, that did. In almost the same motion he used his free right to pound me solid in the stomach.

"*Woof.*" Like a deflated balloon, I staggered back. Fast. But not the kind of fast I'd been hoping was my secret weapon. The fight had begun.

At least he hadn't hit me to the head. I could still think. And what I thought was, *This guy's got fifty pounds on me, easy. Not to mention a clear foot of height. Best keep out of his way.* Which I proceeded to do. I danced around him, ducking and getting off a few weak punches, till I began wondering when the round would be over. Wasn't there some kind of time limit?

The crowd started to boo. It distracted me so that I let the Killer get in close enough to give me another body blow. This one landed me on the dirt floor.

"Time!" Brodie shouted.

I climbed to my feet and swayed till he yelled, "Round Two!" I was learning fast. The round wasn't over till someone hit the dirt.

Round Two was mostly a closer dance with Cohen, locked in a clutch till I thought to kick him in the shin with a heavy boot. Nobody even yelled foul, but the Killer went down with a howl and the round was over. I was just getting into the spirit of Round Three when the crowd noises around me changed. I ignored them. Couldn't get distracted. Did some more fancy dancing, and in the process of ducking a right that would've taken off the top of my head, I felt someone snatch at my suspenders.

"Fight's over, kid. You're under arrest."

"What?"

That stopped me, but the Killer couldn't stop his arm once he'd wound it up. It landed square on that copper's jaw.

"Resisting arrest" was all the policeman said. He shook his head once, as if he got busted in the jaw every night, and grabbed Killer Cohen with his free hand.

Heaving in that officer's grasp, I finally noticed the abandoned seats around the pit; focused on the slight twang vibrating the ropes enclosing us. Looked like the conclusion of my boxing career to me. And not even a five-dollar piece to show for it.

The end of the world and judgment coming.

That's what seemed to be transpiring the morning after. I forced open an eye to the chaos. It was only breakfast arriving, announced by the clanging of a tin coffeepot against iron bars. When I opened the other eye I found myself still in a tight ball and almost stiff as a corpse. Still in jail, too. The cup of weak coffee and slab of dry bread didn't help. When the real judgment came, I was hardly ready for it.

Black Marias delivered the contents of the station house straight to the police court. Inside a courtroom we were lined up in front of the judge, more or less by height. That put me at the front of the line. The judge stared down at me from the bench.

"Your offense?"

"I'm not sure, sir. I think it was fighting in a bout at Brodie's Saloon."

His eyebrows were bushy and gray, and they knotted themselves together in a ferocious line, compounding his glare.

"Not sure? Boxing is barbaric, bloodthirsty, and uncivilized. It is also against the laws of the city of New York, not to mention the laws of the state of New York. Six months in the Tombs should take the fight out of you." He slammed down his gavel.

"Next!"

★ TWO ★

The joint is full, so you get the pleasure of a nice long holiday in Bummers' Hall!"

I already knew to expect the shove the guard gave me, so this time I was ready for it. I also knew about that locking-up sound, the harsh *clank* of bolt against hard metal that shut you away from the rest of the world. I wasn't ready for the huge room spread out before me, though. Arms filled with my official prison kit—a moth-eaten blanket and a set of tin eating ware—I stood and stared. Near to an arena it was, with a high empty ceiling and walls broken by equally high windows letting in a weak, washy sort of February light. Below, long rows of triple-decker bunks marched into the distance, marked off every so often by a lone bucket. Just breathing told you the reason for those buckets.

I wasn't ready for my fellow inmates, either. I gaped for a

long time before it hit me. Then I was back at the bars, kicking and shouting.

"Hey! Hey! You can't leave me in here!"

The guard strolled up and leered at me through the bars. "Whatsamatter, kid? Drunks don't agree with you?"

"But I'm not a drunk! I never even touched the stuff!"

"Let me tell you, after a few months here, you'll never *ever* touch the stuff."

"But, but—" I could almost feel the roots of hair rising on my head, then the red moving all the way down to my face. Yet all that came out in a spate of pent-up frustration was "But you can't even breathe in here!"

The guard was still leering. "Be a good boy and I'll take you out to the Yard for an hour of fresh air this afternoon."

I turned back from the bars, defeated. Maybe the guard watched me wander into that pool of misery, maybe he didn't. All I could do was mumble to myself, like one of the drunks. "Six months of this. For *boxing*. For boxing in one bout at Brodie's Saloon."

The bunks were full, and most of the free wall space had been marked off into separate territories. Dodging besotted men of every age and description—crying drunks, tumbling drunks, blind drunks—I forced myself to cool down and start thinking again. First off, I thought on how I'd get a berth of my own. Next, I wondered how these poor souls could still be besotted, locked away from drink's temptations the way they were. Putting two and two together, I came up with answers and a solution. Wasn't particularly proud of the solution, but I figured first and foremost I'd need to learn how to survive in this hellhole.

Made me a complete circuit of the place, till I spotted what seemed to be the cleanest top bunk. Dumped my gear and scrambled up the ladder to the third tier.

"Excuse me, sir?"

"Wha—"

The owner jerked awake and eyed me blearily past a week's worth of whiskers. "My space. Get outta here."

I reached in my pocket and pulled out the nickel I'd been saving since last week. Saving for something special. It was a shiny one. I flashed it. "Would you consider selling your space, sir?"

The eyes blinked. Then a hand shot up and snatched at the coin. "Certainly."

As he shambled off to bang on the iron bars for some beer, I flipped over the mattress and collected my gear. Top bunk was the nearest I could get to the dirty light filtering down from those windows. It was also the farthest I could get from the sorry dregs of humanity below me. Who'd have thought this was what the Tombs was like. I'd seen it plenty of times from the outside. Everybody called it the Tombs 'cause the builder had designed it to look like some Egyptian mausoleum. I guess the powers that be really wanted you to feel good and dead once they got you inside. They succeeded.

I folded my coat into a pillow and settled in to wait for six months to pass.

"Yard time! Yard time!"

Coming awake fast, I grabbed my coat, and bolted down three tiers to the floor.

"Lockstep for all who's going!"

Two guards stood slapping their clubs into their palms as a short line formed. I expected it to be a ragged one, like everything else around here. To my surprise, the handful of shaky rummies straightened up and stood immediately behind each other, flung a left arm over the shoulder before them, turned their faces to the right and down, and began shuffling in step through the open grate. And they did it all in silence. Not a peep out of any of them. It was strange, but already I'd do near anything for a whiff of clean air. Latching on to the rear of the line, I followed suit.

Outside, when the line broke up, I just planted myself. Took in the hundreds of men milling about the packed dirt of the space between buildings, then closed my eyes and concentrated on breathing. Maybe if I did nothing but fill my lungs for the full hour, it would get me through the next twenty-four. My program lasted for about thirty seconds. That's when I was pushed.

"Outta the way, bummer."

My fists clenched as my eyes sprang open. "Am not a bummer!"

Got another shove for my efforts, this one harder. I spun to face my tormentor. He was a fellow not much older than me. Dark, lean, with a muscular edge and extra inches, too. He smiled down at me and pushed again. Right up close and in the chest, putting a little more power behind it. Without thinking, I let go with my bunched fist, the way Killer Cohen had at Brodie's. Under and up. Right into his jaw. When he crashed onto the hard dirt I spit. "Round One's over," I announced. "Ready for Round Two?"

He sprang up and back faster than I expected. In a moment we were at each other again, with a crowd of interested bystanders forming a ring around us. Next thing you know, *I* was down. Flat on my back, puffing, staring up at those faces. One of them grinned.

"Had all the piss and vinegar taken out of you, kid?"

Tried to find some saliva left in my mouth to make another good show of spitting. Couldn't. I hadn't had anything to drink since that breakfast coffee a hundred years ago. "Not a *bummer*," I managed through dry lips. Then, in an attempt at bravado, "I'm a *boxer*."

The grin changed to laughter. "Not yet, boyo, but the fixings are there." He stretched out a hand to pull me from the frozen earth.

I swayed on wobbly legs, plowing aching fingers through my hair, staring at the man who'd taken an interest. He was at least as old as my pa, and he had that same jaunty top-of-the-world air. But on this man it looked permanent. Medium height he was, with solid muscles flexing beneath his jacket, and a sandy handlebar mustache dominating his round face and bald dome. So why was he in jail? Probably wasn't polite to inquire, but he surely wasn't any bummer.

"That son of a skunk who attacked me?" I asked, for want of anything else to say. "Where'd he go?"

"Skelly? Don't worry about him. He just needed a little exercise." He looked me over again. "Skelly's got the temper, but not the coordination."

I finally managed to spit. Luckily I missed my own boots. "He won, didn't he?"

"He wouldn't of if you'd had a little training. You've got the best natural uppercut I've ever seen." The man stopped, waiting.

I didn't keep him waiting long. I could already tell that being a resident of Bummers' Hall wasn't going to improve my health any—nor my frame of mind, either. A diversion would be useful. "How do I get it? The training?"

The man brightened. He stretched out a thick hand. "Michael O'Shaunnessey at your service. But they call me *Perfessor*. Perfessor Mike. On account of boxing is my game. You could say it's my life."

"I'm Johnny." I reached for the fingers. His grasp was strong but friendly. "You're in jail for boxing, too?"

"Six more months. They cut me out in the very midst of a middleweight championship bout." He shook his bald head sorrowfully. "I was winning, too."

I stared at him. "Why is it the boxers who end up in jail? Why not the promoters?" Scum like Brodie, is what I was really thinking.

He laughed. "Haven't you figured that out yet? It's only *fighting* that's illegal, not hiring fighters. And as long as there's money to be made, and suckers like us to do the dirty work, it'll keep on that way." Then he inspected me closer. "Six months kind of drags around here. I've been looking for some material to train, but Skelly and I never got on. You might make a decent bantamweight with a little meat added to your bones. What do you think?"

I shrugged. "Don't know. They nabbed me in my first fight."

His eyes sparkled. "Novices are best. Haven't had time to learn any bad habits yet."

Sure I was suspicious. Who wouldn't be? Like Pa always said, there's no such thing as a free lunch. But I also wasn't stupid. Anything had to be up from dead time in Bummers' Hall. "When do we start?"

A shrill whistle cut through the Yard. "Lockstep!" was bellowed by a score of guards in unison.

"Yard time's over, kid. Get behind me."

"But don't I have to go back to—"

He gave me a look. "You got anything in Bummers' Hall you can't live without?"

I shivered. "Nothing."

"Then stick with me, boyo. I'll fix it."

"Top bunk all right with you?"

It took me a while to answer on account of I was so busy trying to shut my open mouth. What finally came out was *"Blue blazes!"*

"Not too shabby, eh? All it takes is enough green stuff to cross the guards' palms."

The Perfessor's cell was special, all right: lots of room;

windows; a washstand; furniture and a rug. It even had a pot-bellied stove pulsing heat. That room had everything but freedom. I swallowed and nodded agreement. "Top bunk's fine."

Who'd have thought my saints would take to looking after me in jail? Better than back in the tenements and sweatshop. I swore then and there to start going to mass regular with my ma when I got out of here. In the meantime, I shrugged off my coat and hung it neatly on a hook next to the Perfessor's.

O'Shaunnessey for sure had a little money stashed away. Besides getting the bigger and better cell, he used that money to have special meals delivered. Eggs and bacon for breakfast, with real coffee. Chicken and steaks for dinner and supper. I'd never expected to eat so well in my entire life. But I nearly gagged on my first bite of steak that first night. The Perfessor noticed.

"What's the matter, boyo? Steak too rare for you? I like my meat rare."

"It's fine, sir." I tried chewing again, then stopped. Eating a proper meal again—even if it wasn't the usual boiled potatoes and cabbage—couldn't help but bring pictures of my family to mind. "It's my mother. Ma and the babies. They none of them know where I am. And I would've been paid my wages tomorrow, and the rent's due . . ."

"What about your old man?"

"Pa? Long gone. We manage without him. Least, we did till now. I have—had—a job in a sweatshop. Ma does piecework at home, makes artificial flowers, thousands of 'em. Place looks like a permanent wake." I hacked off another piece of steak with violence. "But it's not enough for the rent. She counts on me." I swiped at an eye, very unmanfully. "And I let her down."

The Perfessor took a long swig of his beer. None for me, though. A jug of specially ordered milk stood by my elbow, since I was now officially in *training*. He took another swig, then stared at me thoughtfully. "What'd you say your name was again? Your proper name?"

I sighed and offered the mouthful. "John Aloysius Xavier Woods."

O'Shaunnessey grinned. "Aloysius Xavier . . . Ax . . . *The Chopper*. Yes. Half the fight game is a good moniker." He wiped beer suds from his mustache. "Johnny 'the Chopper' Woods. Axes 'em down. That'll do." His grin spread. "Gimme your address, Chopper. I'll have my guard, Smitty, run by to see your ma on his way home—with a few groceries and a little rent money. We'll set up a weekly schedule till we're sprung."

I gaped. "You'd do that? For me?"

He slung a hunk of meat in his mouth and growled over it, "Money ain't no good if you can't spend it. You throw a little of it around, by and by it comes back to you."

My rare steak suddenly looked wonderful. I tore into it.

But he made me work for the food, and I soon realized the help O'Shaunnessey was giving my family wasn't charity, either. The Perfessor expected a payback down the line. He was getting just a little old to compete himself, and it was me he was readying for competition. My training began in earnest from Day Two in the Tombs.

★ THREE ★

Up and at 'em, Chopper!" O'Shaunnessey pounded my bunk the next morning. "We'll start you off easy with some wake-up exercises of my own personal devising."

Dawn hadn't even broken yet, and the man was talking *exercises*. Groaning down to the floor, I glanced out the nearest window. It had a real view over a real New York street. Through the gloom you could make out moving shapes—people were out there struggling to their jobs through the wind and a few flurries of snow. If I were still on the outside, I'd be one of those bent-over shapes right now, fighting the gusts on my way to the sweatshop. Another kind of prison. I rubbed my eyes. "Why exercises so early?"

O'Shaunnessey raised his eyebrows. "Didn't think you were that much of a novice. To get the blood moving, of course. We've got a lot of work to do, and only six months to do it in. Watch."

He flung himself onto the rug facedown and started pumping his body up and down. Amazingly fast. Did it ten times, then leaped back onto his feet. He'd already shaven, and his cheeks were ruddy, with enthusiasm oozing from every pore. He wasn't even winded, either.

"Your turn."

Well, it looked easy, but it wasn't. Long before his count of twenty-five I was clinging to the green cabbage-like patterns of the rug, arm and leg muscles quivering, gasping for breath. I managed to swivel my head enough to look up. The Perfessor was shaking his.

"On your feet. We'll have to start off really slow."

So then we worked on loosening up the neck and shoulders, and stretching calf and thigh muscles. By the time he blew out the lamp to let in the morning's light, I was a wreck, wondering if I'd vacated Bummers' Hall too precipitously. That's when breakfast arrived.

Day Three in the Tombs was when it started to snow for good and proper. I noticed it while the Perfessor was trying to teach me how to tell my hands apart after lunch.

"You *jab* with your left. You *punch* with your right. Your left hand is the distraction—" He stopped gesturing from the middle of the rug. "*Not* the snow. Pay attention."

I swung my head back from the windows, wondering what a jab and a punch had to do with life, with the real world going on out there without me.

"Chopper!"

I blinked. "Yes, sir, Perfessor."

The lecture continued. "Your right hand carries the power. Understand?" He held his palms upright facing me. "Now try to hit me. Just my hands, nothing else. Start off with three jabs."

Which one was that again? The left or the right? I aimed both fists for his palms, and what came out was three right-hand pokes.

"Never lead with your right! I said jab! Jab means what?"

I ground my teeth together and blocked the windows and the snow from my head. "Left. Left fist is a jab."

"Correct. Try again."

Up came his palms, out shot my left fist.

"Good." He danced away from me, palms still foremost. "Come after me. Three jabs and a right."

Three jabs and a right. Frowning with concentration, I finally managed it.

"You couldn't break an egg with those punches! Swing your shoulders, your whole body into them. Gives them more force. Again."

Well, that taunt set me off a little, and I gave it another go.

"Improving. But pivot your toes when you swing in with the shoulders. Makes for better balance."

We did it some more, me concentrating on coordinating the footwork with the punches.

"Not bad!" O'Shaunnessey broke for a short breather. "Now I want to hear a good grunt each time you hit me. A proper, ferocious animal grunt."

"What?" My arms dropped. "Why?"

O'Shaunnessey stamped a foot. "You're in the ring, Chopper. You're battling for your life. You want your opponent to think you're a weakling?"

"No, sir."

His hands were ready for me again. "Same pattern. Three jabs and a right. I want to be *scared*."

Sure and I tried to work up some ferociousness, but all that came out of me was a few little hisses along with even weaker jabs.

The Perfessor stopped circling around the rug. "Chopper. You've got to have more anger in you than that. The righteous anger of a tiger kept from his kill!"

I shrugged.

O'Shaunnessey eyed me. "Better yet, think of how you felt every time you added another one of the burn marks to those hands of yours. Think of what you wanted to do to that boss who paid you a nickel an hour to be scarred for life."

"Less," I growled. "He paid me less." Then I went at O'Shaunnessey with a roar. *Jab, jab, jab! Right!*

It snowed for nearly a week with no letup. There was no Yard time at all, and I watched the snow build through our third-floor cell windows. By the end of the week, drifts were blocking the windows of the entire first floor below us. An easy job it would've been to jump out our window into all that nice soft snow, if it hadn't been for the bars. Just jump out the window, struggle through the blizzard, and keep on struggling till a fellow disappeared. Till I disappeared. Forever.

Where would I go? Where could I go? What kind of a future was there for a scrawny half-trained boxer with experience in pressing men's ready-made shirts? Maybe that's the sort of thoughts that had been crossing Pa's mind two years back when he disappeared.

I eased my fingers through the bars and shoved open the window a little. Just enough to poke my nose down for some of that cold, free air. Just enough to grab at a fistful of the snow lining the sill. But when I tried, I couldn't pull my filled hand back through the bars. Had to let go of all that snow to get the fingers back inside.

O'Shaunnessey came over and slammed the window shut. "It won't do, boyo. Freedom's in your head. Set your mind to what's to become of yourself when your time in here is done."

I spun to face him. "How did you know—"

"What you're thinking? Haven't I had the same thoughts myself? And this isn't my first time inside, either."

"But you kept on with the boxing? Even knowing you could end up in jail again?"

"Chopper, my lad, I come from the same tenements as you. Only way out of them is through your brains or through your fists. Since I never got the training to use my brains, I chose my fists." His sober face turned less serious. "It might be your way, too, if I could only get some work out of you. Put up your fists!"

After only a week, the gesture was already automatic. I crouched into the stance, left fist hovering in the space just beyond my nose, right fist guarding my chin—the protective defense of every boxer.

"Good! Now go for my chin. Come on! Wallop me a good one!"

We danced around the rug, sparring in the snowlight. My mind cleared itself of those freedom thoughts. Cleared itself of everything but the here and now of O'Shaunnessey's challenge. I thought sure I couldn't get through his defenses. Thought sure I wasn't anywhere near good enough yet. Then I saw an opening and wound up my uppercut. With a howl of fury I let it go. *Bam.* Right on the chin. O'Shaunnessey stumbled back.

My arms dropped. "I'm sorry! Excuse me, sir. Sure I didn't mean to really *hit* you—"

Then he was scrambling away from the wall and after me again. "Get that defense back in place! Never drop your defense! And *never* apologize for hitting your opponent, boyo. That's the whole entire point of the exercise." He grinned. "But as soon as this blizzard's past, I'm sending Smitty off for a punching bag and some padded gloves. No point whatsoever in destroying our hands—or my jaw—fighting barefisted this way when the sport is heading for gloves."

The snow was long since melted and leaves were budding on the few trees lining the street outside the windows. Week Six in the Tombs. I studied the sight after my regulation one hundred first-thing-in-the-morning wake-up exercises. I wasn't even winded. Turned to the body-shaped punching bag O'Shaunnessey had rigged up in the corner behind the bunks. Pulling on padded gloves, I set in to giving it a proper good pounding. Jab-jab-jab-right. Jab-jab-jab-right. Sharp, fast punches in a rhythmic series. Jab-right-jab-right-jab-right. Then I began with a few combinations. Uppercut, a left hook, pull back for a clean right, and a one-two. I'd started in on another round when the Perfessor pulled me away.

"What?" I protested. "I'm not finished warming up yet!"

"You're warmed up enough for me, Chopper, my lad. It's time for a little strategy before breakfast." He draped a towel over my bare shoulders. "Sit." Spreading a sheet of paper on the small table, he picked up a pencil. "We're going to check you on some theory this afternoon during Yard time. Sort of a test."

"Like in school?"

"Same principle, but I don't think they'd approve of this kind of an examination in school."

I rubbed the towel over my damp head and down my dripping chest. "Who we going to test it with?"

The Perfessor twirled the edge of his mustache wickedly. "Skelly."

Made me laugh with anticipation and glee, that name did. Skelly hadn't let up on me in six entire weeks. Every time I was in the Yard it was "bummer this, and bummer that," along with the prods and shoves that had set us off to begin with. He'd even tripped me once—leaving me facedown in filthy melting snow. The Perfessor said I had to ignore Skelly and all his jibes. Said it was a good lesson in honing my self-control.

I laughed again. It was definitely time to give a little of it back. "Yes, sir!"

"Now, remember my bout I was telling you about? The one in San Francisco back in August of 1879?"

"The one against McClellan! Where you went three hours and forty-nine minutes barefisted!"

O'Shaunnessey grinned. "The very fight. It was grueling, but I survived it using Mendoza's theories—"

"Learn to retreat," I recited. "Utilize side-stepping. Rely on superior agility and speed to win." I stopped. "But when I used something like that at Brodie's, not knowing then what it meant, the crowd booed at me! I think they thought it was cowardly—"

"It's not!" O'Shaunnessey exclaimed. "It's nothing but good strategy. What's the point of just standing there tearing into each other like two bulldogs till one of you drops? Boxing should be *scientific*. It also ought to be graceful, something pleasurable to watch." He smoothed down the neatly trimmed halo of sandy hair around his bare pate. "Also, we got to keep in mind that you're still considerably smaller than Skelly. Retreat and superior agility are needed to keep you alive. But you've got good legs. If you wear him down enough with your dancing to get past his defenses, enough to manage a few well-placed punches, you'll keep your audience's interest. So here's what our strategy is going to be this afternoon—"

The Perfessor was interrupted by a polite knock on our grilled door. He glanced up from the diagrams he'd begun working on at the table. "What is it, Smitty?"

"Sorry if I'm interferin' with the training, Perfessor Mike, but about this afternoon?"

"Yes?"

"We got it all organized with Skelly. Even set up a little ring in the Yard."

"Excellent! What about the bell I ordered? And have you volunteered someone as timekeeper? We're doing this Queensberry Rules—the modern way—after all."

"Everything's taken care of, though some of the boys wasn't too happy about it. They wanted to go the old London Prize Ring Rules, barefisted and no limit to the rounds. But I pointed out what you said about there being not enough Yard time, and they finally let up on me."

"Good work, Smitty." O'Shaunnessey favored him with a smile of approval and prepared to get back to the job at hand. But the guard lingered.

"Me and the boys . . ." Smitty shuffled a bit, then finally spit out what he really wanted to say. "Me and the boys want to know, can we count on Chopper?"

That dragged O'Shaunnessey from his chair. Walking over to the door, he put a hand in his pocket and pulled out a wad of bills. He carefully peeled off a number of them. "I'm betting a hundred on my boyo here." He shoved the money between the bars with a wink. "May I rely upon you to place it for me?"

"No trouble, Perfessor." Smitty lit up with the hope of a good bet. "I'd best be off to spread the word."

"You do that." O'Shaunnessey strolled back to his seat.

As for me, I shuddered for the first time in weeks. "A *hundred* dollars, Perfessor? Do you think I'm worth it? Really ready for it?"

"Got to make things interesting, don't we, Chopper?" O'Shaunnessey gave me his best grin. This time it looked scary. His bland brown eyes turned wolfish. "You'd better be ready for it."

I ducked my head to the sheet of paper and memorized those diagrams like they were the Catechism.

★ FOUR ★

Prison was a lot like a tenement house. They both smelled, they both teemed with too much life, and neither had enough privacy. Back home, when a baby cried upstairs, or to either side of your place, it set off a general round of bawling that seemed to feed on itself. You knew it when old man Kelly came home drunk and beat up his wife and kids by turns. Knew it when Kelly and the missus made up again, too. Didn't need any newspapers to get the news in a tenement. Didn't need any in the Tombs, either.

So why was I surprised when O'Shaunnessey and I broke out of lockstep in the Yard that afternoon to find what must've been every prisoner inside suddenly outside? Even most of the bummers. Maybe it was the day. A special day it was for the middle of March. There was a softness to the air. That little patch of sky showing between buildings was the most elegant blue, with a few puffs of white clouds marching across it. Maybe it was thoughts of seeing the first few dande-lions that hadn't been trampled into the dirt bursting into a yellow brighter than the sun.

Then again, maybe it was me. Me and Skelly.

The crowds broke open like the Red Sea to let the Perfes-sor and me walk through. They backed off in silent, staring columns to either side, making a passage to the promised land waiting beyond: the ring. The carefully roped-off ring in the center of the Yard.

The Perfessor lifted the ropes for me to slide under. He watched me shrug off my shirt and snap my braces back up. Then he pulled the gloves from the kit he'd been carrying. Held one out for me to slip into.

"This is it, boyo. What we've been working for. Do me proud."

"Yes, sir. I'll try, sir."

O'Shaunnessey's eyes caught mine. Their brown had gone a sharp, almost steely color. "Trying isn't good enough, Chop-per. Not today."

"No, sir, Perfessor." His tone chilled me as I slid fingers into the second glove and flexed. Then I raised my eyes to the far side of the ring. Skelly was still on his way, making his own entrance past shouts and slapping hands. The prisoners liked Skelly the Thief, considered him one of their own. Could be he was. Could be O'Shaunnessey and I were in too tight with the guards, had it too easy. But it was the first ease I'd found in my life. Maybe I hated Skelly for more than his bullying. Maybe I was a little jealous of his stealing his com-forts while I'd been slaving my guts out in the sweatshop, not knowing what my true way was. Yet we'd both ended up in the Tombs.

Skelly was still coming on. I lifted a padded glove to my face and took in the fine smell of soft leather. Maybe this would be my way, after all.

It took Skelly an eternity to get past his cheering comrades and skip lightly over the ropes and into his corner. Then he was stripping all the way down to dark blue boxing tights, making me feel like the beginner I was in my worn old trousers. His second fitted his gloves. Suddenly it wasn't an eternity anymore. There he was, leering at me across the ring. I clamped my mouth shut tight and waited.

Pretty soon an old convict who looked as if he'd been in the Tombs forever groped his way under the ropes and to the center of the space. He held up a hand and the crowd slowly simmered down to silence.

"Prime day for a bout, gents." He swiveled his head toward windows in the far corner of the inner building. Up to where we all knew the warden kept his office. He waved. "Prime day for some *exhibition sparring*, I mean to say. Got to keep everything *legal*, right, gents?"

General hoots of derision followed.

"Do your refereeing, Burton!"

"Get on with it!"

Burton snickered and got on with it. "So here on this prime day we got four rounds of *exhibition sparring* coming up. Queensberry Rules. That means a gloved contest of three-minute rounds. One-minute rest between rounds. A ten-second count in the event of a knockdown . . ."

Burton waited for the yells of enthusiasm to die down.

". . . And no wrestling or blows below the belt." He turned toward Skelly. "Now, in this corner we got the Pride of Five Points, looking to be about five foot, nine inches, mebbe a hunderd and forty pounds. Lemme hear it for Tommy 'Tough Boy' Skelly!"

A roisterous shout built over the Yard. Skelly pummeled his gloved fists at the sky and did a jig to the noise of the crowd. It went on so long that the guards pushed their way through the prisoners and repositioned themselves around the ring.

Burton finally raised his own arms to calm the mob. "And in this corner"—he turned to me—"at about five foot, four inches, possibly a hunderd and ten pounds, we got the Bummers' Best, Johnny 'the Chopper' Woods. Lemme hear it for—"

This time it was boos that ascended into the afternoon sky. I didn't think it was fair bringing up that Bummers' Hall business again. Not at all. Not after surviving six weeks of constant scoffing from Skelly. Six weeks of keeping a tight lid on my temper. I made a stab at patting down the red hairs prickling with anger at the back of my neck, then remembered I had the gloves on. In full spleen, I turned to O'Shaunnessey leaning against the ropes beside me. "Why—"

O'Shaunnessey gave me a bland look. "You can't take it, you don't belong in the ring."

"Whose side are you on?"

But then Burton was bawling out one last thing. "All right, you two: meet at the scratch, shake hands, and get on with the fight!"

I swiveled toward the center as a bell rang, a tinny little clapper bell. Pushing out of my corner, I met Skelly in the middle. Tommy "Tough Boy" Skelly. Skelly the Thief. Skelly who'd first called me a bummer and never let up since. We slapped gloves, then without even thinking, I worked up a howl, lunged right in, and hit him with a left hook to the head. An angry left hook. The Pride of Five Points wobbled, then crumpled to the dirt.

"Four . . . five . . . six . . ."

Burton was bending over Skelly, making the knockdown count. I hovered in the nearest corner, ignoring the screams of outrage rising beyond the ring. Ignoring the outstretched arms of the guards holding back furious prisoners. Skelly didn't look great lying there. Strands of black hair fell greasily over the spreading bruise high on his cheekbone. Had I really hurt him? Had I—

On the count of seven, Skelly pushed himself to his knees, then was up on his legs again. He gave his head a good shake and came after me with murder in his eyes. I got my defense back up again fast, and over the roars of the crowd I lithely dodged his fists. I kept dodging until the bell rang, then slumped back onto my corner stool with relief.

O'Shaunnessey was all over me, rubbing me down with a

towel, jamming a dipper of water between my teeth from the corner bucket. "Keep it up, boyo. Stay out of his way, but don't lose the anger."

I managed to catch the Perfessor's eye for a split second. I spat out the mouthful of water. "You planned it this way, you probably even set up that 'Bummers' Best' . . ."

O'Shaunnessey grinned, and the bell sounded. Round Two.

This time I was spitting mad at O'Shaunnessey for taking advantage of my sore point. Skelly's dark, thin head rounded before my eyes. His slim torso thickened. He was looking more and more like a cross between the Perfessor and our punching bag. I ducked and went in low, under his guard, jab-right-jab-right-jab-right-jab-right, a crisp staccato just beneath the ribs. Then I pulled back fast. The rest of the round went like that, with Skelly picking up on my tricks. We were both bobbing in for hits, then running. When the bell sounded again, Skelly and I were dripping with sweat, but he was heaving harder than I was. He'd had to do a lot of dancing to keep up with me, and I don't think Skelly'd been exercising for the past six weeks the way I had.

O'Shaunnessey's old grin was back in place as he worked me over. "Keep it up, boyo, and you'll earn a piece of my winnings."

I spat again. "This isn't about winnings. Not anymore."

It wasn't for Skelly, either. We were hell-bent on knocking the stuffings out of each other. As Round Three began, he came straight for me, mean and lean again.

"*Bummer,*" he growled through his teeth. "Gonna fix you this time. So there won't be enough pieces to send back to the drunks."

Somehow, somewhere, Skelly had found another wind. Maybe he'd found something else, too. There was something odd about his gloves. They were glistening, as if his second had spilled water over them. Had a funny feeling about those gloves. Trying to get out of their way, I found myself up against the ropes for the first time. And Skelly was going for my face. I slipped down and missed most of the blow, but he still managed to glance my head, near my left eye. A smell wafted past my nose. Almost like . . . *turpentine*! He'd doused his gloves with turpentine to blind me!

Still on bended knees and outraged, I forced my right into a killer uppercut—directly beneath Skelly's guard and straight into his stomach. He staggered back, freeing me from the ropes. Time to get my head working again. Time to use some of that strategy the Perfessor had been beating into me. But Skelly rebounded sooner than I expected. He was crowding me again, back toward the ropes. My gloves went up to my head. My fear of being blinded overtook everything else. When Skelly couldn't get near my head, he got me in a clutch and raised me bodily—half into, half over the ropes. Then he leaned. Hard.

This was one mean customer. Meaner than I'd thought anyone could be. Skelly was fighting dirty. First the turpentine. Now he was trying to break my back—and he had the weight to do it.

The bell rang. Burton had to tear Skelly off me so I could

stumble back to my corner. *Blue blazes!* Where'd I be without those Queensberry Rules!

"What happened out there?" O'Shaunnessey was upset. Not near as much as me, though.

"Turpentine," I panted. "On his . . . on his gloves."

"Filthy bastard! I'll put an end to this right now!"

"No!" I grabbed for the Perfessor. "Let me . . . let me finish him. Just one more . . . round."

O'Shaunnessey wiped the sweat from my face. The towel came away stained with blood, too.

"Sure you can handle this, kid?"

"Chopper," I growled. "The name's *Chopper*."

I was already up as the bell sounded. Up and after Skelly and those lethal gloves of his. Only three minutes. Just three minutes more and the fight would be over. I went at Skelly with legs and fists churning. Went at him like the bulldog the Perfessor had been scoffing about. No more blasted dancing for this fight. My jabs flew over Skelly's hands and arms, a straight right punch went for his head. A nasty left hook went foul in his kidneys. The crowd roared. Did some side-stepping to catch my breath, then went at him again, feeling my wrath coming through the punches. Knew it wasn't right, but couldn't do a thing about it. Boxing was meant to be scientific, but Skelly's freshly gleaming gloves had nothing to do with the science of the sport. And those gloves were coming closer again.

I dodged and circled, letting him come after me. When I saw weariness pushing back the bloodlust in his own eyes, I closed in for the kill. My uppercut to the jaw. I sucked in some breath and let out a roar that spoke for all the heat of rage in me. Matched it nicely with the uppercut. Skelly toppled and was still out for the count when the bell rang.

Then I was staggering, standing between O'Shaunnessey and Burton the referee. They were holding up my gloved fists. High. Burton was trying to shout something over the roars of the crowd. I finally heard it through the ringing in my ears.

"And the winner is . . . Johnny 'the Chopper' Woods!"

It wasn't boos that registered on me next. It was a steady, incessant chant:

"Chop-per! Chop-per! Chop-per!"

I finally managed to turn to O'Shaunnessey. He grinned down at me. "Congratulations, boyo. *Now* you're a boxer."

★ FIVE ★

Month Six in the Tombs. I had a sack filled with my few belongings and a stack of old *Police Gazette*s and *Leslie's Illustrated*s, ready to go. The Perfessor swore by—and over—their boxing stories. I gave the cell one last glance. It'd been too empty the last few days with O'Shaunnessey freed before me. Then I walked to the door and gave a whistle for Smitty.

He bustled up the corridor, fussing importantly with his ring of keys. "The big day at last, eh, Chopper?" The door creaked open and I stepped out.

"Sure is, Smitty." I searched my pocket to find what I'd saved for him. Held out the five-dollar gold piece. "Thanks for looking in on my ma all this time, Smitty."

"Say, it wasn't nothing. She's a fine woman. And Perfessor Mike paid me fair and square. Still, it's white of you." He took the coin fast enough. It disappeared inside his uniform tunic and he led me down the corridor, down the steps, and to the exit of the Tombs at last. At the threshold, Smitty lingered long enough to clap me on the shoulder. "You're welcome back anytime, Chopper."

I smiled. "Thanks for the invite, but I think I'll pass on it."

Then there I was, on the streets of New York. A free man. First thing, I filled my lungs with a deep breath of the muggy August air. It smelled wonderful. Next I felt for the small lump in my trousers pocket. Ninety-five dollars in bills. What was left of my piece of the Perfessor's action on the fight with Skelly months back. It was my starting-off money. Something to keep me and the family going until I figured out what to do with the rest of my life. It wasn't bad pay for six months. Not bad at all. I picked up my sack and set off to finish what I'd started doing six months ago: get home to my ma's hot supper.

"Johnny! Johnny!"

Multiply that times six, add a few tears, and kids screeching and clinging all over me, and you get a picture of my homecoming. So did the rest of the tenement, probably. I finally managed to pull off the little ones—like ticks, one at a time—to give my mother a proper hug. She felt smaller, and there were new strands of gray mixed through the dark red hair of her bun.

"Thanks be to all the saints," she was crying. "You're home at last, and safe. It's so good to look at you."

"Thanks, Ma. Same here."

Then she pushed me away to really look.

"You're different, Johnny. You've grown right out of your clothes!"

I glanced down at my trouser legs. They stopped a good three inches above my ankles. Wasn't the sort of thing you spent much time thinking about in prison. "Guess I'll have to get me some new duds."

"And you've filled out!"

"The Perfessor fed me pretty good—"

Ma was studying my face now. "Johnny! Are those whiskers?"

I could feel the blush building to red already. "Come on, Ma, enough. What's for supper?"

She made a nice retreat. "What's usually for supper, son? Cabbage and potatoes"—she paused to smile—"and corned beef! God bless Mr. O'Shaunnessey."

"Amen to that." I manhandled Jamie under one arm, his twin, Katie, under the other, and, surrounded by Bridget, Liam, and Maggie, pushed through the usual mounds of artificial flowers cluttering the kitchen to get at the table.

I'd been back two days and had barely managed to catch my breath. I spent some of my savings on a new set of clothes that fit, and boots that didn't pinch, and outfitted the little ones likewise. When we arrived home from that excursion, Ma was sitting at the kitchen table in one of the new dresses

I'd forced her to buy, surrounded by the stems and buds of a hundred paper flowers. The kids tore open their parcels and began showing off their windfall.

"Johnny!" Ma exclaimed. "All that money you spent!"

"They needed shoes, Ma. And decent jackets for winter. Now Maggie and Bridget and Liam can start in on school next month without being ashamed. They need to go to school. They can't be hanging around here helping you with the flowers for the rest of their lives. And it'll be a little easier on you with only the twins to look after."

"But Maggie and Bridget—and even Liam—are getting good with the flowers. The girls have a way with them, almost artistic, it is." Ma smiled with motherly pride. "And we'll be needing the extra earnings now that Mr. O'Shaunnessey's money has stopped coming. The rent's due again—"

"You'll not be worrying about the rent, Ma. *I'm* taking care of things—everything—from now on." I reached into my pocket with a flourish and slapped a ten-dollar bill, a month's rent, on the table. Ma stared at it.

"How much is left, Johnny? Enough for next month, too? Enough for next week's bread and milk and potatoes?"

"Course there is." I confidently dove back into my endless treasure trove and scattered what was left over Ma's bits and pieces of flowers. We stared at it a moment, then I fumbled in my other pockets. Came up with three pennies and a dime.

Ma was straightening the bills, piling the coins. She sighed and looked up at me. "Six dollars and thirty-three cents, Johnny. That's what's left after the rent. Out of the ninety-five you came home with."

I rubbed my head, mussing the fine new haircut I'd treated myself to. Then I rolled down the sleeves of my new shirt, and carefully buttoned the cuffs; cast around for where I'd cavalierly tossed the well-cut suit jacket that would complete my sartorial splendor. "I guess ninety-five dollars doesn't go as far as a fellow would think these days, not with seven people to outfit. I'd best be off to find myself a new job."

"Oh, Johnny." Ma sighed a second time. Her forehead wrinkled. "You'll not be getting yourself arrested again, will you? And will you be back for supper?"

"No to the first, and I don't know about the second. Feed the little ones without me."

I had to wait while Maggie and Bridget proudly modeled their new school pinafores, and Liam his knickers. Then I was out of the stifling heat of the tenement and into the swelter-ing heat of the city, scuffing my new boots over the sidewalk. Too big for my new boots, I'd gotten. Too big for my new britches, too. Swaggering around the way I'd been, spending money as if it were water. Spending my entire emergency sav-ings in two days. Acting like some conquering hero, when the entire world knew it was only jail I'd come home from. Only from the Tombs.

Even feeling as low as I was, I knew I wouldn't be going back to any sweater's shop. Couldn't. There had to be something better in life than slowly dying behind locked doors and filthy, closed windows for twelve or fourteen hours a day.

Truth to tell, I wasn't crazy to go back inside any room for a while. Even our two-room flat. The walls just seemed to start closing in on me. What I needed was some outside work. Something where I could use all those muscles O'Shaunnessey had given me.

So I prowled around the city, noticing things I hadn't noticed before. Maybe I hadn't noticed them for the very reason that I had been locked away inside for so long. Two years at the sweatshop when I had to leave school after Pa's desertion. I'd even made it to the eighth grade—the first in our family to get that far. My shoulders shrugged of their own accord. And probably the last, the way things were going . . . Then six months in the Tombs.

I raised my head to the sky to remind myself that I really was out of prison. But it wasn't the sky I saw. What I saw was all the wires sprouting from hundreds of poles that had risen in my absence—like leafless trees, they were, lining the streets. Telephone wires, I knew. For the swells around Wall Street. Hadn't ever seen a telephone, but people talked about them, talked on them. And electric wires, for all those new lights they were starting to turn on every night up and down Broadway. Hulking above the wires were the tracks of the el, shadowing everything below. I stopped and rocked with the vibrations as a heavy steam engine chugged right over my head. At ten cents the ride, I'd never been on that, either. Never had the need to go where it was going. All the way north past Central Park to Harlem. Or across the shiny new Brooklyn Bridge to what lay beyond.

Brooklyn. Those long nights in the cell when we'd lay

sprawled on our bunks in the dark, O'Shaunnessey would talk. How the man could talk, as if he'd kissed the very Blarney Stone itself. But then, he'd been everywhere, seen everything. He said nothing in his travels was as nice and cozy as Brooklyn, though.

"I tell you, Chopper, if I were the settling-down sort of man, it'd be Brooklyn I'd do my settling in. You can rent a complete house there for only twenty dollars a month."

"Twenty dollars? That's only twice what we pay for our two rooms in the tenement! Why doesn't anybody know about it?"

"You think the slum landlords want to lose their incomes? You think they want to advertise that a man who saves his coins could be doing more than renting cheap just across the bridge in Brooklyn? He could be *buying* himself a house for only six hundred dollars. Lock, stock, and barrel."

"You mean things like a yard—"

"I'm talking porch, yard, even grass, boyo. Just like the rich swells."

O'Shaunnessey's words came back to me as I moved out from under the el into the sunshine again. A whole complete house with a yard, and grass, and space out back to grow your own vegetables—or flowers. *Real* flowers. I smiled. Ma would love that, all right. Real flowers instead of everlasting artificial ones. Space for the little ones to get some air instead of being cooped up in the tenement all day 'cause Ma was afraid to let them out—

I was so full of my thoughts, I stumbled on something, almost fell.

"Open your eyes and look where you're going, buddy!"

"What?" I came back to earth on the very edge of the earth, at least a great hole. I swayed like a bummer for a moment, then managed to pull myself back to safety. Only then did I take the chance of peering into the huge, long ditch. "What're you doing?"

"What's it look like?" a begrimed fellow called back up, his head on equal footing with my boots.

"Digging to China?"

"Ha! Got us a comic here, Al," he yelled to someone below. "Thinks we're digging to China!"

"Send him off to a vaudeville house, then, and get back to work, Ben."

I sank to a crouch and peered deeper into the mysterious hole. "For sure, what are you doing?"

"Laying pipes for Mr. Thomas 'the Genius' Edison's steam heating system, is what."

"If he's such a genius," Al complained, sending a spray of dirt onto the dike above him, "he should think up an easier way of digging."

This was fascinating. "What's Mr. Edison going to heat?" I asked.

"Offices for all them high-toned nobs in the business district around Wall Street, come winter."

"Does he need any help?" I stopped. "I mean, do you need any help? Digging."

Ben shrugged his shoulders. "Talk to the foreman." He pointed. "Up ahead half a block."

"Thanks! Thanks a whole lot!"

I removed myself from danger and strode up the street flexing my muscles. This was a job I could handle. This was a job that would keep me in trim when O'Shaunnessey looked me up again, the way he'd promised he would our last day together. And why wouldn't he, after all the effort he'd expended? Surely it wasn't just to pass jail time. So all I had to do was get myself a decent job, keep fit, and wait. I arrived at the next clump of sweating workers and asked after the foreman. A giant of a man unbent from the piping, wrench in hand, to glare at me.

"You got him. And I'm busy. Get on with it."

"Work. I'm looking for work. I'm strong and willing." I flexed my muscles to prove the point.

"Strong enough to keep up the pace for ten or twelve hours a day?"

"Yes, sir!"

"Who do you know?"

I took a step back. "What do you mean?"

"Who do you know down in Tammany? At City Hall?"

That made me blink. "Nobody."

"What about your alderman?"

"I'm sorry, but—"

He waved me off. "You look all right, but these are patronage jobs. You gotta be appointed, gotta pay your dues. Come back when you know somebody."

I could feel my very muscles shriveling beneath my new shirt and jacket. Patronage? Paying my dues? To get a decent job I had to be in politics? It would be a cold day in hell before I got a job here. I stumbled away from the ditch and Mr. Edison's steam pipes.

The answer was the same at every construction site I visited the rest of the afternoon and long into evening. I headed back to the East Side as the sun set and storm clouds began moving in from the ocean. In desperation I even knocked on the doors of two sweatshops. They were slammed in my face by men speaking broken English. Too many foreigners were arriving off the boats. Too many people willing to work for next to nothing. The price of cloth was rising, the profit margin falling. No work.

As thunder rumbled over my head I found myself on a familiar street, standing outside a familiar building, staring at a familiar sign. But something about it was different. I read the sign again:

BRODIE'S SALOON AND BOXING CLUB
MEMBERS ONLY!
EXHIBITION SPARRING NIGHTLY
$5 PURSE TO 4-ROUND WINNER!
LIKELY LADS INVITED

As lightning cut across the darkened sky, I clenched my fists, shouldered the door open, and strode inside.

★ SIX ★

The fug was the same. So was the sawdust. This time I didn't waste my efforts with the bartender. I just pushed my way through the men holding up the bar to the door beyond. A brute of a fellow was blocking it, ham-like arms folded in warning. Probably just graduated from the gangs. I'd seen his kind back in the Yard, all brawn and few brains.

"Membership card," he growled.

"Since when has Brodie's gone uptown?" I asked.

"Since the last couple of raids. Cops been getting greedy and Brodie's been losing pugilists faster'n he can get 'em in the ring."

"So calling it a *club* changes that?"

A nod. "Makes it all hunky-dory."

"Meaning legal."

"Yeah, *legal*." He snorted.

"But business as usual?" I asked, just to be sure.

"Business as usual."

I broached the final question, the obvious one. "How do you join the club?"

"By passing me a buck."

"Kind of high, isn't it?"

"Not when the cops get an even split to keep off our backs."

"Ah." But I had no money, anyway. Not even a nickel in my pocket like the last time. I fully intended to come away with some, however. I straightened my new inches. "I've got business with Brodie, so I won't be needing a membership."

"Whyn't you say so to begin with?"

The bruiser moved aside with annoyance, and I entered the pit.

The cockfights were in full progress. I ignored the flying feathers and deadly spurs to hunt for Brodie. He was jammed into the aisle seat of the front row of his bleachers, smoking a cigar about a foot long. Couldn't miss his carefully tended head of steel-gray hair, or his overfed belly.

"You still looking for boxers, Mr. Brodie?"

"Hey?" He pivoted his head and Havana in my direction.

I raised my voice over the din of the crowd. "Need a fighter for tonight?"

"Always need a fighter." The cigar bobbed as he inspected me from the neck down. "Bantamweight?"

"Yeah."

"Take all comers? Any size?"

"You bet."

Brodie considered. "Got a moniker?"

"The Chopper."

That seemed to sit well with him. His lips curled around the cigar. "What's your record?"

"One draw, one knockout." The draw part wasn't exactly a lie, since my bout with Killer Cohen had been interrupted. "The knockout in my favor," I added, just to emphasize the point.

His stone-black eyes lingered a moment longer, then he made his decision. "You're still early on, but we'll give you a shot." He jutted his chin to point the cigar. "Around the pit and through the last door. You'll get a shout when it's time."

"I know," I answered, but he didn't hear me. Didn't remember me, either. Just let out a puff of rank smoke and directed his calculating eyes back to the fighting cocks.

I went through the final door recalling my last time in that back room. How scared I was. How dumb. Dumb and desperate. Maybe not so much dumb, I thought to myself, as unschooled. I glanced around. Was I being worse than dumb this time? Or just plain desperate again?

There were a fresh bunch of fellows stripped down and limbering up. I stripped and joined them. Started in with O'Shaunnessey's first-thing-in-the-morning wake-up exercises, even if it wasn't morning. Like he always said, it got the blood moving. By the time I pulled myself off the floor from a hundred of those, all five fellows were standing in a circle, staring.

"What?" I asked, without a puff.

"That was amazing," one of the fellows proclaimed.

"Never saw anything like it," offered another.

"Um," tried a third, "would you mind showing us how to do it? It's not a secret or anything, is it?"

I coolly surveyed the group. "Where's Killer Cohen?"

The smallest fellow, about my size, but thick around the neck and chest, answered. "Still doing time."

"In the Tombs?" I asked. I didn't think so. I would've seen him there.

"Nah, he pulled a whole year. Got sent up to Sing-Sing on account of slugging a copper."

"But that was an accident!" I exclaimed, without thinking.

"How would you know?"

This time I thought first, but spit it out anyhow. "I was there. I was his opponent."

"That means you . . ." The short fellow backed off a little, wary and respectful both. The others did, too. So being a graduate of jail carried prestige in certain quarters. I shrugged it off.

"Yeah. I got six months in the Tombs. I've been out two days." A new thought hit me. "If he hasn't replaced the Killer, Brodie really has to pay out for each fight, doesn't he."

I grinned as they nodded. They didn't seem like a bad bunch. Maybe a little cooperation would sweeten the competition in the pit. Maybe it would also reveal their strengths and weaknesses.

"Say, let me show you the trick to doing Perfessor Mike

O'Shaunnessey's finest exercise of his own private devising—"

"Mike O'Shaunnessey? The retired middleweight champ?"

"Him that fought with John L. Sullivan himself?"

"The same," I was pleased to answer. "We're acquainted, and I really don't think he'd mind. You." I pointed at the short one. "What'd you say your name was?"

"Didn't, but it's Bill. Bill Bullock. They call me 'the Bull.' "

"Good enough. Down on the floor next to me, Bull, and I'll demonstrate." Then I was down on the floor with him, going through the pumping motions slowly and carefully for willing students.

The warm-up in the back room put a whole different cast to the fights at Brodie's that night. It surely changed my frame of mind. I still wanted to win, but I was no longer willing to maim anyone for a five-dollar purse. The anger just wasn't there. Somewhere along the way of doing those exercises most of my desperation disappeared.

The anger wasn't there for the other fellows, either. We performed more like a team, more like in real exhibition matches, waltzing around and showing off techniques to each other. Course, somebody had to win, and I wasn't loathe to be that somebody. And I had been using my head, studying what the fellows had to offer. After putting the Bull down in the fourth round with a strenuous right to his wide chest and wide-open belly, I did pretty much the same to a taller guy who called himself "the Tiger." I made him growl, all right, mostly in pain. But no serious harm done. Brodie came into the ring as we shook hands after the call.

"Chopper." The voice was thick and hoarse. His cigar waggled, down to a mere stub now.

"Yeah?"

"Here's your purse. Both purses."

He handed me two five-dollar coins. I bit them just to be certain they were good. With Brodie, you never knew. "Thanks, but what about the next bout?"

"Eight rounds from you will do for tonight. Got to keep the betting spread. But come back tomorrow night, with gloves." His black eyes flickered. "I'm changing over to Queensberry Rules. Guys are all wrong, they think it's for weak brothers. Get those fists protected, you can do some real damage."

Wasn't sure I approved of his motives, but I liked the idea of fighting with gloves again. I sucked on my battered knuckles. Liked it just fine. I also liked being invited back again.

"Sure thing, Mr. Brodie."

I got back into the night to find that the storm had cleared the air. I strolled home through puddles of rainwater, enjoying the cool breeze, feeling the bruises starting in to ache, but also feeling alive. Wonderfully alive. I let myself into our fourth-floor flat quietly, knowing everyone would be long since asleep. Negotiated through piles of flowers to drop my jacket over a kitchen chair . . .

"Johnny?"

"Ma?" I turned toward the lumpy sofa, our one piece of real furniture left over from slightly better times. "Go back to sleep, Ma," I whispered. "I'll just get my blanket from the bedroom. I'll bunk up on the roof tonight."

"It is heavy," she murmured, "even after the storm."

"That comes of only the one window in here, and none in the bedroom. No ventilation." I moved toward the back room as quietly as I could, having no desire to wake all five little ones curled up inside.

"Johnny?" Ma was at it again.

"What?"

"Did you find a job?"

That stopped me. "Sort of. Yes and no."

"That's no answer, Johnny."

"We'll talk in the morning."

I fetched the blanket and escaped to the roof as fast as was possible. Coming through the trapdoor, I peered into the starlight. It was as crowded as Bummers' Hall up here. Everyone who could leave their kids alone for the night had. Couldn't let the children sleep up here, though, even for a breath of air. There'd been too many had rolled over and off the roof's edges in the middle of the night. Not a nice sight on the sidewalks first thing in the morning when you went out for milk and bread.

I shook the grisly image from my mind, found an unoccupied spot, and settled down to sleep. But then I couldn't. A hot bath was what I needed after eight rounds in the ring. A massage like O'Shaunnessey said as how the professionals got after big fights would've been welcome, too. I twisted within the blanket. My muscles didn't seem to want to settle down. I felt all jumpy. And how in the world was I going to explain to Ma that our rent money would be coming from Brodie's Saloon until I found some better piece of work? How was I going to explain that what had sent me to the Tombs was going to be feeding all seven of us?

"Stop kicking! A man needs his sleep!"

"Sorry." I apologized to the bundle next to me and settled down more quietly. At least, my body did. My brain kept right on kicking. Ten dollars for one night seemed like an amazing amount of money. But there were expenses involved. I began tallying them. The gloves I'd have to buy tomorrow. And food. Couldn't expect a boxer to live on soggy potatoes and cabbage. Couldn't expect him to fight on it. To keep my strength up, I'd have to start the day with eggs, like O'Shaunnessey always did. And there'd have to be some meat thrown in along the way.

Maggie and Bridget and Liam and the twins paraded before my eyes. They were scrawny, too, the way I'd been before the Perfessor. Too scrawny. Funny how I'd hardly noticed that before in any of us. They'd be needing meat and eggs, as well. And Ma was looking too tired since I'd gotten home . . . I drifted off counting how many bouts I had to fight to make all these new ends meet. How many bouts I could survive. Small wonder Pa had taken off.

★ SEVEN ★

Things didn't get much clearer in the morning. The day started right enough, but that's because I stayed up on the roof till everyone else had gone off to their jobs. I was waiting to have the space entirely to myself. Weren't many spaces a fellow could have to himself in the city of New York. Then I set in to my exercises. They weren't something I wanted to do in our flat. Wasn't even enough clear floor to spread my new length out there.

Getting through the starting twenty-five of those wake-up exercises was almost as bad as the first day I'd done them back in the Tombs, I was that stiff and sore. Things improved after the second twenty-five. By the end of the hundred the moving blood actually felt good. When I finished up with the rest of the limbering, when my body began feeling like a well-oiled machine again, I headed directly down five flights and onto the street. Buying a dozen eggs, fresh bread, and butter made me feel good, too. It was what came next that kind of cast a pall over the day.

"A dozen *eggs*? And *butter*?" Ma stared at the largesse.

"You do know how to cook eggs, don't you, Ma?"

"Of course I know how to cook eggs!" she snapped. "What I don't know is how we can afford them."

"We have to afford them. It's part of my new . . . work." Somehow I couldn't say *job*. Nothing anyone did at Brodie's Saloon seemed clean enough to be considered a legitimate job. Ma didn't notice the word choice. She was still staring at the eggs.

"You need to eat a *dozen* eggs?"

"No." I sighed. "There's seven of us, right? One for everybody, a few extra for me, and maybe you can make a cake or something with the rest."

Liam wandered out of the back room, rubbing his eyes. "Cake?" His eyes widened. "Is it Christmas?"

That innocent remark told me how far we'd really sunk. I slammed the fresh loaf on the table and went to the basin to strip and wash. "There's going to be a dozen eggs every morning from now on, Ma," I snarled. "And I need four of 'em. Fried or scrambled, I don't care. Just get used to it."

"Johnny!"

"What?" I turned at the anger in Ma's voice, water sloshing down my chest.

"Johnny." The anger turned to sadness. "You sound just like your father."

I stood there dripping, feeling like Ma had taken the belt to me. No. It wouldn't have been Ma. It would've been Pa. I'd almost forgotten about Pa's rages. I didn't want to be like that. Didn't want to be like all those red-faced men throwing their wages into Brodie's pit, either. I dripped all the way to the nearest chair and slumped into it. Wooden slats cut into my back and my head sagged.

"Sorry, Ma," I mumbled. "I truly am. I just didn't know what you'd think—or say." I rubbed at my damp head and forced my eyes up to meet hers. "Thing is, it looks as if I'll be working nights, and I need my strength."

The rest of the kids had woken by now and were standing solemnly between Ma and me, wondering what was coming next. I finally gave them the truth. "I tried so hard, but there's no jobs to be had." I stretched damp fingers into my pocket and eased out one of Brodie's five-dollar pieces. "Look. I made that last night boxing. At Brodie's Saloon. He wants me back for more tonight." I pulled my attention from the golden coin. "It's something I can do, Ma. It's something I'm good at."

Ma's eyes left the coin to stare at the bruises turning black and blue all over my bare chest and arms. I'd forgotten about them. "Is it worth it, Johnny?"

"It's what I can do, Ma."

She took down a skillet from its hook on the wall. "Then I'd best start in on your eggs."

I took Liam with me when I went off in search of gloves. He'd kept staring at me all during breakfast. Staring through those bright blue eyes set in the thin face under a mop of red hair. A perfect duplicate of the rest of the family. Even after Ma plunked a shiny yellow fried egg in front of him, he kept staring.

"Eat your egg, Liam," I ordered. "It'll make you big and strong."

"Like you?"

"Yeah." I tried on an O'Shaunnessey-style grin. "Like me."

He ate his egg. Out on the streets we found the gloves at Peck & Snyder's Sporting Goods; then I bought another two shirts so I could have something fresh to wear to work between laundry times. I found a spare penny in my pocket to buy Liam a stick of peppermint candy and we walked down to Battery Park to inspect progress on the Statue of Liberty going up across the harbor. We found a mangy old ball someone had left behind and tossed it back and forth for a while. Then we headed back home. The final stop was a poultry shop. I bought a freshly plucked chicken and Liam proudly lugged it home by its legs. Back in the kitchen he tried to lift it high enough to drop on the table.

"Stop!" Ma shrieked. "The flowers!"

I managed to wrest the bird from his grasp and set it in the dry sink. Liam stuck his hands in his pockets and beamed.

"It was the best day I ever lived," he declared. "Better than Christmas." Then he began listing in gruesome detail every blessed thing we'd done, topping it all off by pulling the ratty ball from his pocket. The other kids got more and more jealous and upset. Wasn't anything to be done but go the whole hog.

"All right, then," I said. "As long as I've got the night work, I'll take one of you out each day. Everybody gets a turn. Understand? Until school starts and as long as I've got the work."

Ma stood up from the table. "Things seem to be changing around here" was all she said. Then she began dealing with that chicken.

Things started to change at Brodie's, too. I ended up boxing about three nights a week. I needed the time in between to let my body heal a little from the pounding it took. And I never boxed more than eight rounds—sometimes less, if I managed an early knockout. Couldn't skew Brodie's betting scheme, could I?

At first the competition wasn't too tough, and I got to thinking about it as if I were going onstage each of these nights, just like the Perfessor told me he used to during his exhibition tour of the country a few years back. I began enjoying matching my body against the opposition, comparing my tight muscles with their untrained brawn; figuring on how my shorter reach could be used to my advantage; falling back on my knowledge of Mendoza's theories when the heat turned overwhelming. So add it up, and there I was, bringing home a steady thirty dollars a week, for three entire weeks, right up to September.

But like I said, things started to change. First it was the competition. Somehow, Brodie was beginning to attract more professional fighters. Bull and the Tiger didn't bother coming around anymore trying for rematches. I had to fight harder for my wins, harder for my money. I had to fight more aches and pains and sprains, too.

And then there were the crowds. They seemed to be changing as well. The beery workmen began to be shoved aside by better-dressed uptown types. The crowd sounds changed, too. Over the regular cheers and boos, another sound came to my ears. I tried not to let it break my concentration, but after a while I couldn't help but notice what they were shouting:

"Chop-per!"

"Chop-per!"

"Chop-per!"

Just the way they had after my fight with Skelly in the Tombs. That's when I figured it was time to have a little chat with Brodie.

I cornered him between the rats and the roosters one night at the beginning of my fourth week.

"Chopper, my boy!" He slapped me on the back, beaming around his ever-present cigar. "What can I do for you?"

No point in beating about the bush. I came right out with it. "Seems like your customers are starting to change. Seems like the crowds are beginning to come out to see *me*, Mr. Brodie." I took a deep breath and finished the thought. "Seems like it's time we talked about a raise."

The tip of his Havana rose. "That's what it seems like, is it?"

I squared my shoulders. "Yeah." Couldn't quite make myself say "Yes, sir," to Brodie. I didn't have either the trust or the liking for the man.

"And what might you be considering a more equitable arrangement, then?"

"Double," I said. "Starting tonight."

"Double." The cigar waggled. He clapped my back again. "Done."

That's when I knew I was worth more. That I should have asked for more. Wasn't a matter of greed, was a simple matter of value due for merit. Value due for putting my body and health on the line too many times a week, too. Even John L. Sullivan spread his real fights over a longer period of time. Over months. What I needed was either a manager I could trust, or some education. Since I hadn't heard a peep from O'Shaunnessey in the four weeks since we'd parted ways—since maybe, it was beginning to dawn on me, I'd never hear from the Perfessor again—I figured perhaps it was the education I would have to go for. Just enough education to judge my own worth. But first I had to survive another night in Brodie's pit.

When the girls and Liam started school a few days later, I walked them straight to the door and into their classrooms. I made good and sure their teachers knew to expect them each day. Made good and sure the teachers knew they weren't just any tenement kids. Someone was responsible for them. Someone would be right there at the end of the school day to hand-deliver them home. Then I kept on walking another block to the high school, meaning to sign myself up for classes.

The four-story, dark brick building loomed before me. Peaks and towers decorated its roof, while rows of windows stared expectantly. There were only about a dozen steps running up to its wide front doors, but suddenly the thought of climbing those steps scared me silly. I shoved my hands into my pockets, where they turned into fists. I was a boxer. I lived by my muscles. What right did I have to enter this building? I turned away.

Three more days I came back to those steps and thought about the impossible height of them till other students, normal students, began staring at me. When I took notice, I saw that they weren't so much different after all. They wore the shabby clothes and had the lean, hungry look of neighborhood kids. I finally steeled myself to mount those steps.

Inside, nothing looked that special, either, except for what was being offered. Turned out to be what they called a vocational school—a trade school aimed at making useful citizens out of tenement toughs. I didn't mind a little education in machinery and carpentry. What I was really after, though, was the reading and writing and arithmetic, even if they called them fancier names after eighth grade. So I got a list of books, bought them, and settled in to try and keep my body still for about seven hours of classes a day.

It should've been easier to do than managing much longer days in the sweatshop, but it wasn't. I'd gotten accustomed to spending a lot of time outside, either on the roof with my training, or taking the kids for their one-by-one adventures.

In just three weeks these adventures had expanded. Liam was still satisfied with his stick of candy and ball-playing at Battery Park. The twins were, too. Maggie and Bridget were a different kettle of fish. They wanted to ride on the horsecars or the el. They wanted to get off to look in the windows of fancy uptown shops. On Maggie's last excursion before school, she wanted to stay on the horsecars all the way up to Central Park. I was beginning to feel uncomfortably like some out-of-town tourist, but humored her anyhow, so we sat on the car until we came well into the park, next to a big barn of a building sitting in the middle of open fields.

"What's that, Johnny?" she asked.

I craned my neck to read the lettering on the red brick building. "Says it's the Metropolitan Museum of Art." I settled back on the bench. "In a few months you'll be able to read that, too."

And why not? Maggie was clever. She was also nine years old. She should've started school years back. Somehow I just hadn't been noticing things all that time in the sweatshop. I was the oldest. I should've noticed things. If Patrick and Brendan had lived, there'd have been brothers almost as old as me to help with the noticing. But the influenza had taken them so long ago, I could hardly remember them anymore—

"Johnny!"

Maggie's shove brought me back to the here and now. "What is it?"

"What's a museum?"

"I guess it's a place where they keep old things to show people."

"Can we go in? Will they let us in?"

"I don't know."

"Well, they have to let somebody in, don't they?"

"I suppose so."

"And I'm wearing my good school pinafore today."

I smiled. "You are at that."

"Make the horses stop, Johnny. I want to go in that museum and see what there is to see."

I stared at my sister. Not only was she clever but she had a mind of her own. We got off at the next stop and walked back. I read the sign outside. "It says it's a free day, Maggs. Let's try it."

Turns out the Metropolitan had a statuary hall filled with marble statues. Naked marble statues. Mostly female, but a few male ones, too. I couldn't help but do some gawking. Those female ones were a little scrawny. Lovely Lucy and Delicious Delilah back at Brodie's Saloon could've pounded them into the dirt in under a minute with their Fists of Fury. The statues of the gods were more impressive. I stood sizing up a fellow called Apollo, flexing my biceps, figuring on how many rounds we could go—

"Johnny!" Maggie was pulling at me. "There's more in the next room. Different things."

"Aw, Maggs."

It was an exhibition hall stuffed with relics from some ancient country. Then Maggie dragged me upstairs, which was filled from floor to ceiling with the most amazing paintings. Lots of good pugilistic material there, too. We stayed until they threw us out in closing.

Outside, I shook all those new images from my head and started worrying about finding a horsecar to get us back home before Ma decided we'd been kidnapped and abducted to the opium dens of Chinatown. But Maggie, she just stood on the weeds by the side of the street. Her face was scrunched up in thought. She finally shared what was troubling her.

"Johnny."

"Yes?"

"Oh, Johnny! That's what I want to do. Make art!"

I stared at her a long time, digesting that. What I finally said was "If I can be a boxer, I can't see any reason why you can't make art, Maggs."

The horsecar finally showed up.

All through this time Ma kept on producing artificial flowers. I tried to get her to stop. She'd only look at me and say, "I know exactly what to expect from these flowers, Johnny. Can you say the same of your boxing?"

I shook my head. "No, Ma, I never know what to expect of anything anymore."

★ EIGHT ★

September disappeared into October, then into November. It got too cold to sleep up on the roof nights, so I had to bunk on the floor by the kitchen table. My head always ended up lodged against one of the bushel baskets of apples I'd taken to hauling home while apples were still in season. It was a nice smell, though, and it was even nicer to crunch into one while I was bent over the kitchen table working on my schoolbooks the nights I didn't have to go to Brodie's. Maggie and Bridget and Liam hunched with me, doing their own homework. They were all of them taking school seriously, I was pleased to see. By November, Maggie was already reading up a storm. She was also scratching drawings on every spare scrap of wrapping paper that came into the house. The girl was preparing for school holidays over Christmas. She fully expected those excursions to start right up again. Expected me to take her back to that Metropolitan Museum of Art.

"You said as long as there wasn't school, and you were still working, Johnny."

"Maggie's right," Liam piped up. "You promised, Johnny."

Ma sat at the far end of the table, piecing buds and stems together. "Johnny's already doing far too much, children. You can't expect everything."

"He did promise!" Bridget exclaimed. She wanted another visit to those department stores.

My pencil stalled over a nasty bit of arithmetic: determining gear ratios. It felt like I was being pulled apart again. Too many people wanted a piece of me. Too many ideas, too. I never knew there was such a thing in this world as Shop Mathematics. Nor sentence diagramming, either. I frowned at the thick copy of Swinton's *Grammar* lying in wait for me. Mrs. Rosen, my English Grammar teacher, said she was really teaching mental discipline. She said the mind was a muscle, like any other, and it needed exercising, too. But how you exercised it by diagramming sentences like "Be a hero in the strife" hadn't dawned on me yet. Predicates and nominatives and modifiers were giving me more pain than a sharp hook to the head.

I rubbed my brow where it ached. And here I'd thought English class would just be giving me a little extra reading along the lines of the *Police Gazette*. At least that always had an article or two on the latest fights . . . And when all this math and grammar was done, I still had to write an essay. An *essay*. Three pages long. In proper grammar and handwriting.

My fingers came into focus. Proper handwriting from scarred fingers and swollen knuckles? The subject to be something I knew about. What did I know besides the tenements and the Tombs and Brodie's? *Be a hero in the strife.* Sure.

The kids were still clamoring.

"Wait till Christmas comes, then we'll see."

Meanwhile the money was piling up, almost as fast as my bruises. Ma still thought I was making ten dollars the night. I let her keep thinking that and hid the other half safely away in a bank for eventualities down the road. In the here and now, I wanted to rent a bigger place so I'd have somewhere to sleep, somewhere for a little privacy during the wintertime, but Ma put her foot down.

"We've managed in the flat this long, Johnny. I won't be going into new expenses until we have a real nest egg, something to tide us over. You've taken to the schooling and I'd like to see you continue with it. What happens if you lose your work at Brodie's?"

What happens, indeed. The whole entire family's expectations had risen considerably since this time last year. It seemed to me that prison—and boxing—had had quite a lot to do with it.

My second bout at Brodie's the next night—Friday night— Brodie matched me up with a brute known as "Juice." I didn't think I'd lost weight since the Tombs, but I hadn't gained any, either. I was steady somewhere between one-twenty and one-twenty-five, and Juice looked to be about two hundred. Maybe I'm exaggerating, but Brodie kept no scales to prove me wrong. Granted I was still fast, but a slight fellow—a bantamweight—needed speed *and* a miracle to go up against this kind of opposition. Brodie must be hedging his bets again, placing money against me in hopes that I'd lose.

When the bell rang for the first round, I knew I'd have to win this one on points. There was no way I was going to knock Juice either over or out. We slapped gloves and I got out of his way fast, then figured I'd make him chase me, tire him out. Heavyweights tired out fast. So I did some fancy dancing. Stopped. Did some more. Stared. Juice hadn't budged. He just stood there rocking in the center of the ring, looking mean. And stupid.

Blue blazes. Somebody bigger than Juice had given his noggin one punch too many. Had to be. I scooted in, under his defense, and did a little rat-a-tat-tat on his ribs. Scooted back out. Nothing. No response. Darted back again, tried the same play. His right fist rose like a sledgehammer and aimed straight down for my head. I retreated fast. One blow from that fist and I'd be out of the fight. Probably out of this world.

"Hey, Juice!" I skipped in from the side and you could see the thought it took for him to even turn his head. By that time, I'd circled around his back, leaped up, and landed a hard right to the other side of his head. He fell, like a tree.

"*Tim-ber!*" the crowd bellowed.

I pulled back and made for a neutral corner, not believing my luck. The shouts began again, building and building, drowning out the long count over Juice:

"Chop-per!"

"Chop-per!"

"Chop-per!"

Someone was leaning over the ropes, tapping my back. Brodie.

"Hey, kid."

"Yeah?"

"After you're changed, I wanna see you upstairs. In my office."

"Sure."

I'd never been upstairs, never seen Brodie's inner sanctum. All the way up the dark flight of worn steps I went over in my head what the man could be wanting. What he needed to say that couldn't be said in his usual place of business, the pit. Would he offer another raise? Somehow his voice hadn't had that sort of sound to it. I finally made it to the top, paused, and knocked.

"Enter!"

I entered. The place was small and crowded. Just Brodie's huge desk piled with papers you could've blown the dust off of, and Brodie behind the desk, flicking two inches of ash from a fresh cigar into a spittoon by the side of his chair.

"Sit." He pointed at the only other chair in the room. I sat. Waited.

"So," he began. "You got yourself a record. Unbeaten."

"Yeah." It hadn't been easy, either. Especially not lately.

"Suddenly we got more and more nobs coming all the way from uptown to grace my joint—coming to see you."

"That's what it looks like."

Brodie puffed on his cigar. He eased the smoke out slowly. "I don't mind the added class. Not at all. But I still got a situation of diminishing returns on my hands here. People say you can't lose. I give you tougher competition to improve the odds. I bet on the competition. You don't lose. *I* lose."

I almost said "Sorry," then cleared my throat instead. Why should I apologize for winning?

"It's time we came to an understanding, Chopper."

I shifted in the chair. "What kind of an understanding did you have in mind, Mr. Brodie?"

"What I had in mind was you fighting again tomorrow night. Saturday night. My biggest night."

I flexed my muscles. Hadn't taken too much of a beating in the pit tonight, just a few hard jabs to the chest in the first bout. "I could do that, Mr. Brodie."

"That's the first thing." He puffed again. "Second thing . . ."

"Yeah?"

"Tomorrow night I want for you to lose."

My whole entire body stiffened. "Lose? On purpose?"

"Call it anything you like. Call it the end of a long winning streak."

That's when I felt my temper—Pa's temper—rising in me. It hadn't happened for a long time. I hadn't felt those pinpricks from the back of my neck, working their way down. Hadn't felt the red rage start in me. I gripped the arms of the chair, but didn't say a thing. Brodie noticed.

"For a payoff," he added.

"How much?" Heat was almost steaming from my ears. In a moment I was sure it would be visible, as visible as Brodie's cigar smoke. But I needed to know what Brodie thought my soul was worth.

He unplugged his Havana and licked his lips. "A hundred bucks."

"That's all?" I almost screamed it. Losing naturally was one thing, and even I knew that someday I'd lose naturally. But losing *on purpose*? That's all it was worth?

"All right, two hundred bucks. That's my best offer."

For once my mind was working as fast as my temper. Maybe all that grammar was helping. Two hundred dollars was what most working men made in a year. It would put me in the position I'd been striving toward. Striving toward so secretly that even I was scared to put a name on it, for fear it might all fall through. It would put me in the market for a house, a little cottage in Brooklyn. It would get Ma and the kids out of that lousy tenement forever . . . It would also make me feel rotten. My knuckles gripping the armrest had turned white. I nearly pushed myself out of the chair, then forced myself back to cool off and think some more. Sat there and watched the blood flowing back into my tensed fingers.

Wasn't it my duty to do the best thing for my family? I took a deep breath. Considering it that way, was it really my soul I'd be selling? Blast it all. I was almost ready to sell it right then and there for some decent advice. The kind of advice the Perfessor could give me. And where was *he* when I truly needed him? He'd up and disappeared from my life as quickly as he'd entered it, leaving me with a single skill, but no future. And he'd promised me a future. My anger suddenly turned from Brodie to O'Shaunnessey. I wanted to hurt him. Bad. I said, "Make that three hundred, and you've got a deal."

"Two-fifty," Brodie shot back.

"Done." I pushed from the chair before I changed my mind. Stretched out my hand, palm up. "I believe you owe me for tonight's fights, Mr. Brodie."

He grunted, pulled out a wad, and peeled off my pay. "Nice doing business with you, Chopper."

I took the last of my honest money and left.

The floor felt harder than usual that night. I tried to soften it by painting pictures in my head of the private room and comfortable bed waiting for me in that Brooklyn cottage. It didn't help. I woke up sore and short-tempered when Liam stumbled into me while reaching for one of the last of the apples in the basket behind my head.

"What're you doing?" I yelled.

He jumped back, eyes wide. "I was hungry, and it was too early for breakfast, and—"

"Take it and get back to your room!"

Liam scuttled away, and I ducked under my blanket again, but it was no good. The whole day was as rotten as the last of those apples. The family steered as clear of me as they could, and I almost saw them sigh with relief when I took off for Brodie's.

Things didn't improve there. When I slipped under the ropes for the big fight, the packed crowd started in on their chant early, before my opponent was even announced.

"Chop-per!"

"Chop-per!"

I ignored them and turned to the fellow who was going to beat me tonight. Brodie'd been smart. He hadn't sent this one to the back room beforehand. I sized him up as Brodie did the intros. Mick "Griffo" Griffin. Maybe one-thirty-five or -forty, good strong calves and thighs, solidly developed chest and biceps, all topped with a thick neck and a shock of curly black hair falling around a broad face. I gave Brodie more credit. Griffo looked to be a fairer competitor than usual. My fall wouldn't seem obvious.

The bell rang.

Griffo came at me with determination, and I matched him. Had to put on a good show for at least a round or two. That's what I told myself. Put on a good show, but don't take too much guff. Why get hurt when you were being paid to lose anyway? That's what I told myself. But then I got involved in the fight, the way I always did. Shut out everything outside the ring and concentrated. Made my own little world between just the two of us. Lunge for a jab, bolt from his return, lunge for a combination. Griffo was good. When the bell rang again, they had to pull us apart.

Brodie was waiting outside my corner. He pulled out his

cigar to growl in my ear. "Looking good, kid. How about in Round Three?"

I nodded, hardly hearing. I was busy focusing on Round Two. The bell sounded and I was up again. Doing the work I knew how to do. Doing the job O'Shaunnessey had taught me. Griffo's broad face changed into the Perfessor's for a moment, the way Skelly's had in that fight in the Tombs. He was grinning. "Keep it up, boyo," he said. "Make me proud."

Make him proud. I went for the smile with a sharp, straight right, wanting to wipe out O'Shaunnessey's grin forever. I connected with Griffo's mouth instead. My punch jerked his head aside, and I knew I wasn't really fighting O'Shaunnessey anymore. Wasn't fighting Griffo, either. It was myself I was fighting. I'd been trying to do something, get something, the easy way. I backed off from a natural follow-through opportunity and let the boos from the crowd filter in. Should've figured it out by this time. Should've known that for me there'd never be an easy way. I took a deep breath and headed back for Griffo. He'd had time to recover, but I pounded right through his defense anyhow. Pounded with all the frustration building in me since last night. Brooklyn would have to wait. There was no way I was taking a fall for Brodie. I just didn't have it in me.

Griffo never had a chance against my demons. He went down before the bell and stayed down.

Brodie's face was not a pretty sight. He didn't invite me up to his office again. Didn't even wait for me to leave the ring. His voice was hoarse and low as he leaned over the ropes, but it came through the jubilant stamping and screaming of the crowd loud and clear.

"You're history, Chopper. Walk outta here now before I get my boys to carry you out in pieces."

All right, I'd known the run had to end sometime. Yet all the way home I played that last scene over and over in my mind. Huddled into my coat against the early December cold, I worked through it like the rounds of the fight itself, searching for a different outcome before the bell.

What if I'd honored the deal with Brodie? I'd have had two hundred and fifty dollars in my pocket now, this very minute. Tomorrow I could've taken Ma and the kids on an excursion to Brooklyn to study the real estate. By Christmas we'd have had the best present of our lives.

The picture faded, like my future. I shut it down before I could kick myself. Something had happened to me back in that ring tonight. I'd made a decision. Maybe deep down I'd always known the truth. I'd lose one fight, everybody would say, "Well, the kid had to fall sometime." Then next week, or next month, Brodie would ask me to do it again. It would be easier the second time. Easier still, the third. Taking a fall into hell.

I burst into the flat still tense, and stopped short. The lamp was lit, and Ma was sitting on the sofa with little Katie in her lap. Katie was coughing her lungs out.

"What's the matter, Ma?"

She stared at me, hopelessness in her eyes. "It's been going around, Johnny. The Kelly kids have it and the Donohoes. The Fiorellis, and the O'Reillys, too. Katie started tonight after you left, full-blown."

I'd been unbuttoning my coat, but I closed it again. "I'll go fetch a doctor."

"This late at night, Johnny? Who would come to the tenements?"

"They'll come when they see the color of my money."

"Money doesn't cure everything. Wait till morning, Johnny."

Ma probably had a point—several points. I had a night more wretched than the last, and by morning Jamie and Bridget were coughing, too. I never told Ma about losing my job. I just went in search of a doctor.

It was the whooping cough, the doctor said, which might disintegrate into the scarlet fever. And not much could be done about any of it, aside from pouring thick cough syrups and chicken soup down the patients' throats and keeping them as cool and dry as possible. The authorities didn't even bother quarantining the place, and within a few days you could hear whoops echoing from one floor to another, down one long hallway to the next.

"Fresh air would help, too," the doctor had said.

But where could you get fresh air in the tenement? Only places like Brooklyn had fresh air.

The last thing he'd said as I paid him was "Some survive it, some don't."

★ NINE ★

It must be a wonderful thing to have the foresight. Knowing the future would have made it a whole sight easier to sell my soul to that devil, Brodie. As it turned out, I was stuck with my decision and my guilt, stuck with the other hell we were all now living in.

Katie, Jamie, and Bridget all had the whooping cough bad, and fevers, too. For a wonder, it seemed to pass right over the rest of us. That was a blessing, because the rest of us were needed for the nursing. Ma spent every minute she wasn't cooking chicken soup curled up on the sofa with one child or another in her lap. She'd be comforting them, easing them, crooning to them, all the time a string of rosary beads worked its way through her fingers. While I was carting sheets to the laundry and buying new ones to use in between times, Maggie kept hot water boiling and went from one patient to the next, wiping them down. When that didn't work, I went out again and hauled back a block of ice. Liam pulled Ma's copper washtub out from under the table for me and I set the ice into it, then the two of us chopped off pieces to wrap in towels to bring down the fevers.

I was the go-between from the tenement to the outside world. Pretty soon I started thinking about the other families surrounding us. The ones who couldn't afford the chickens or the syrup or the ice. The ones who couldn't splurge on the Chinese laundry for the first time in their lives, the way we'd been forced to. The agony floating through those halls was such that you couldn't help but think about the others.

I started with extra chickens and cough syrup, knocking on doors and making the offer.

"Could you use a chicken for some broth, Mrs. Kelly?"

"You'd be Mary Woods's boy? Johnny?"

"Yes, ma'am. Can you use the chicken for your little ones?"

"God bless you, I could."

Knocked on another door, the O'Reillys'.

"Could you use some cough syrup—"

"Johnny Woods!"

So there I am holding up a bottle of nasty black stuff that'd make you want to vomit just looking at it, and who opens the door but Maureen O'Reilly. Hadn't seen her since we made our First Communions together. Well, I'd seen her some in and around the place, but she'd always sort of bob her head and look the other way. A lovely head it was, too. Shining black hair. And skin paler than china. Black Irish. I stood there holding up that bottle, feeling the red return to my face, feeling like the freckles I hadn't been blessed with were surely popping out of my very pores.

"I heard tell you're a famous boxer now, Johnny."

"It's not true," I mumbled. I wasn't any kind of a boxer anymore. Not since last Saturday night. "Do you have a need for the syrup?"

She reached out for the bottle, then dropped her hand. "O'Reillys don't accept charity, Johnny. We never have, and never will."

"It's not charity!" I exploded. "It's helping when I'm able, and the helping's needed." O'Shaunnessey's words from so long ago came back to me. They spilled out. "Money ain't no good if you can't spend it. You throw a little of it around, by and by it comes back to you."

Her hand hadn't budged. "You have that much money to throw around, Johnny?"

"No!" There was the Perfessor, getting me in trouble again. "I mean—" What did I mean? "Maureen O'Reilly, I know you've got sickly little brothers in there. Swallow your pride and take what's being offered!"

She took it and slammed the door in my face. I looked down at my empty hands. I'd given away all my offerings. Couldn't give more where it wasn't wanted. I went back home.

Just before Christmas a black van started pulling up in front of the tenement steps each morning. I'd stare out the window, watching the matching black team of horses stamp and toss their heads, watching the parade of small bundles being carried down the steps in silence, being set into the van. The parade was worse on the way back into the building. That's when the keening would begin. Keening fit to make you clap your hands over your ears. All those little souls were gone from the tenement forever, gone to a better place with the Lord in heaven. It was poor consolation for those left behind.

For our own household, it was touch and go. Little Katie was the worst. I thought sure we'd lose her too many times. In the end, maybe what saved my sisters and brother was the fact that they were better fed than the others at the beginning of the sickness. Maybe my boxing work—the training diet O'Shaunnessey had taught me and I'd forced on the family— had been useful for something. Then again, maybe it was God and all His saints listening to Ma's unending prayers and deciding to look after us.

We survived, and with the survival was reborn in me a stronger urge than ever to get my family as far away from the tenements as possible. As soon as possible.

I never got to finish the end of the school term when things calmed down, but started searching for work again instead. I had to. The sickness and the charity had dug a hole in our savings. It was a few days before Christmas. I soon learned that a few days before Christmas was not the time to look for work. But the prime of summer hadn't been, either. Or maybe I was just being too choosy. After Brodie's, the idea of slaving for less than a nickel an hour no longer appealed to me. More than that, it made no sense.

So I put on my suit and tie and searched for work at higher-toned places. Places where I could truthfully write on the application that I'd had some high school education and was maybe capable of doing higher-priced work. By Christmas Eve, nothing had come of the effort. I quit my search early and devoted the rest of the afternoon to spending money I could ill afford to spend.

For Ma I bought a new rosary, because she'd fairly worn the old wooden beads to nubs over her Hail Marys for the little ones. For Maggie I bought a tablet of good paper and a set of colored drawing pencils. For Bridget I found a pretty little shirtwaist blouse the likes of which she'd been admiring in those uptown windows. Liam got a new ball and a baseball bat—although I did hesitate over those particular choices. It meant I'd also be promising more time down in Battery Park, time I wasn't sure was going to exist. The twins got a doll and a little train engine that tooted when you wheeled it across the floor. Ma would probably be doing more than blessing me for that toot after Christmas wore off.

Loaded down as I was, I still managed to add a small crate of oranges to my parcels. They would be healthy for the kids still recuperating. Job or no job, I figured we deserved to celebrate this Christmas. We were all still alive.

The day after Christmas, the morning of my sixteenth birthday, I dressed up in my finest again and set off to make the rounds of all the places where I'd left those applications. The answer was the same from all of them:

"You look like a fine lad, but we need more than just half a year of high school. We need a certificate of graduation."

A certificate of graduation. A diploma. Pa probably would've sneered at the very idea. A *real* man worked with his hands, in Pa's estimation. Well, I'd tried working with my hands in the sweats. Then I'd tried working with my fists. It was only those few months back at school that'd made me think about working with something else. Developing that muscle Mrs. Rosen kept going on about. Working with my brain. Hadn't O'Shaunnessey said that was the other way to get out of the tenements? But school took time, time I no longer had. That one missing piece of paper was probably going to keep me down forever.

How in the world was I going to support the family, and continue high school, *and* get us out of the tenement? The odds were stacked against me. There's no way Brodie or his crowd would ever bet on me now.

Trudging despondently up to the fourth floor on my return home, I almost bumped into Maureen O'Reilly coming down. She smiled.

"Johnny! Your syrup helped, I'm sure it did. I *know* the ice you left with my ma helped. Billy and Joey are getting better. They're going to make it!"

"Swell, Maureen, I'm happy for you." I pushed past and continued my climb.

"*John-ny!*"

My name turned into a wail floating up the stairwell. I ignored it to shove open the door to the flat. Didn't have time for any more complications right now. Especially not female complications. And pretty as she was, Maureen was definitely female.

Our recovering patients were draped all over the sofa, and Ma was at the table making artificial flowers again. Maggie and Liam were helping. Almost a relief that was to see. At least something was back to normal.

"No luck yet, Ma." Wearily I began shrugging off my coat and jacket, when I noticed something new, something different.

Propped up against the table's centerpiece—Pa's old beer growler filled with a bouquet of finished flowers for inspiration—was an envelope.

I stared at it, wondering. "That envelope . . ."

Ma glanced up, her fingers never stopping their labors. "It came while you were out, Johnny. A fellow delivered it. It's for you."

My coat fell to the floor as I reached for it. Sure enough, there was my name on the front. Mr. John A. X. Woods. Never got a letter before. I fingered the envelope. The paper was thick and cream-colored. I turned it over. There was printing on the back, fancy engraved printing. "The *New York Athletic Club*? What in the world would be coming for me from the New York Athletic Club?"

Ma sighed. "Sure and you could try opening it to find out, Johnny."

I did. After slitting it open, I pulled out a single sheet of equally rich paper. Unfolded it. Finally I read it.

Chopper,
Welcome home, boyo! Even if it is a belated welcome. It took me a while to sort myself out, but I finally landed in the gravy but good. Got myself taken on as official Boxing Master of this fine establishment. If you can stand mixing with the swells that frequent the place, stop by for a visit. We need to talk about your career.

It was signed with a flourish, "Michael O'Shaunnessey, Professor of the Science of Boxing."

Every bit of resentment left in me flew straight out the window. O'Shaunnessey hadn't forgotten me after all! I smiled, then I laughed out loud. "Looks like I've got to go out again, Ma. It's from the Perfessor at last, and he wants to see me. Maybe for a real job."

Ma finally set down the wires she'd been twisting into stems. "Mr. O'Shaunnessey? After all this time? And will it be the fighting again? You've barely healed from that work at Brodie's—"

"There's no telling, Ma. With the Perfessor you never can tell." I poured half a cup of coffee from the pot sitting on the stove and gulped it down. It would warm me for the weather outside. Not that I needed that much more warming. Already I felt on fire with anticipation and hope. Maybe there was still some promise left in my fists. "All I can say is that it *won't* be like Brodie's. Not a bit!"

I set out from the tenement, a totally new man from the one who'd trudged home only an hour ago, and walked at a clip uptown to the New York Athletic Club.

It was a long haul. The club was situated on prime real estate at Sixth Avenue and Fifty-fifth Street, a far cry from the Bend and the rest of the Lower East Side. I hesitated outside the fancy doors, suddenly glad I still wore my suit and tie. I paused to straighten the tie. Would they let me inside? Well, wasn't anything for it but to try. I climbed the steps and pulled open the door. There was a guard sitting just inside. He looked me over.

"This is a private club. Members only."

I squared my shoulders. There was more there to square than when I'd last seen O'Shaunnessey. "I'm here by invitation." I pulled the envelope from my pocket and waved it. "By invitation of your new Boxing Master."

"Perfessor Mike?" His scowl disappeared. "He's up in the gym. Let me show you the way."

Then I was walking past acres of marble and polished wood, smelling the smell of expensive cigars drifting from side rooms. It looked like O'Shaunnessey had landed in the gravy sure enough. Upstairs and through more doors, the space suddenly opened into a gymnasium so incredible that I felt my knees sagging.

"*Blue blazes!*"

The walls went several stories straight up to the ceiling, which opened to a skylight. Climbing ropes floated down from that ceiling, and strange machines cropped up here and there on the floor below. They were tempting, but I ignored all of them for what I saw filling the center of the room: a ring. A regulation boxing ring, like I'd seen pictures of in the *Police Gazette.* And in the middle of it was O'Shaunnessey himself, cheerfully sparring with a weedy-looking fellow in fancy exercise gear. I trotted closer to the ropes, then waited for the end of the round. It came with the shrill ring of a bell—an electric bell. My head shook with the sheer extravagance of it all. O'Shaunnessey glanced over.

"Chopper! Just the man I needed to see!"

Tongue-tied, I listened to his greeting. It was as if we'd parted only yesterday, not nearly five long months ago. Those few words were all I needed to hear to complete the healing. How could anyone stay mad at the Perfessor?

"Strip down, boyo, and go a round or two with young Wells here for me. He's about worn me out."

Still wordless, I stared at the Perfessor, then Wells. If anyone was worn out, it was Wells. O'Shaunnessey looked as if he could go another fifteen rounds easy. But I stripped. I owed the Perfessor more than one favor. When I was ready, O'Shaunnessy slipped under the ropes and held them up for me to take his place. He gave me a broad wink, a wink Wells couldn't see.

"Go easy on him, lad. Nothing rough." Louder, he said, "Use my gloves."

I was a little rusty. It had been over three weeks since I'd shown my back to Brodie and his money. Three weeks with little time for anything but nursing. But when the bell shrilled again, I was ready.

Wells wore a protective leather helmet over his head, and a sort of breastplate to guard his chest. Glancing down, I saw he'd also strapped on a groin pad. Small wonder he was out of breath, carrying around all that armor. Never even knew the stuff had been invented. I moved in to give him a little exercise.

Afterward, when Wells had politely thanked me and gone off to the changing rooms, I leaned against the ropes with the Perfessor. He gave me an inspection almost as good as that first afternoon in the Yard at the Tombs.

"I'm pleased to see you've kept yourself in shape all these months. You did a nice job with Wells, Chopper. Gave him an easy workout without making it look easy. He went off happy with himself."

"Is that what you do here, sir? Make all these rich swells happy with themselves?"

He grinned his old grin. "You got it in a nutshell, boyo. And for this they pay me good money."

I considered. "How do I get some of that good money, sir?"

He pulled at his mustache. "That's what I've been thinking on. You've built up some good muscles, but you're still a little young for professional competition, still need experience—"

"Stop." I held up a hand. "I'm not a novice anymore, Perfessor. There's been a lot of water over the dam since Skelly. I've had more experience than you would believe. Too much experience, in fact."

His eyebrows rose. "Want to tell me about it, Chopper?"

★ TEN ★

I launched into a blow-by-blow account of my experience with Brodie's Saloon—and Brodie. I gave O'Shaunnessey the works. It was the final attempt at bribery which got to him.

"That dirty, no-good cockroach! Tempting you. Trying to take you down to his level. That *scum*! That son of a—"

He stopped short. His brow wrinkled all the way up to his bald crown.

"Undefeated? Did you say you were *undefeated* for all those fights, Chopper? Every single one of them?"

I breathed a sigh of relief. It hadn't been easy confessing how close I'd gotten to becoming Brodie's kind of scum. "Seems like it, Perfessor."

O'Shaunnessey studied me again. Then he whistled, long and low. "Maybe we got something here. Maybe *you* got something. Something even more special than I estimated."

He worried his mustache a little. "This calls for some heavy thinking. Under the circumstances I don't want to go rushing into anything until we work out a plan. A good plan."

"What about in the meantime, Perfessor?"

"The meantime?"

The telling of the story had taken long enough to cool me off from the rounds with Wells. I gave my bare chest one more swipe with the Athletic Club's thick towel and reached for my shirt. "In the meantime I have a family to support, and money I owe you—"

O'Shaunnessey waved off the latter. "Not to worry about anything I spent in the Tombs, Chopper. As your manager I'll get a piece of any action, right off the top. That'll be payment enough."

I nearly didn't catch the rest of what he said, because I almost stopped breathing when he said the magic word. *Manager.* "You'd be my manager? You'd be willing—"

O'Shaunnessey clapped me on the back, not at all like Brodie used to. Then he held out his hand. "I'd be more than willing. Gentleman's agreement, Chopper?"

We shook. "Yes, sir, Perfessor. Gentleman's agreement."

We stood there grinning at each other for a while, until O'Shaunnessey finally spoke again.

"However." He looked me over yet another time. "We still have the meantime to consider. How to keep you in shape, and you and your family well fed."

And there I was, holding my breath again. Would he have something for me to do? Something honorable?

"It just so happens that the powers that be here at the club want me to set up a series of exhibition bouts. A couple of nights a month. Bring in a few outside lads, let them have a go at each other for fun, let the members throw around some of their excess cash on side bets—"

"Yes?" Sure and I was going to turn blue soon if he didn't get to the point. He did at last.

"I don't see why you couldn't be part of that crew, Chopper. It'll keep you in trim for bigger things down the line. It'll give us the chance to plan. Might be worth a few bucks, too."

"Got to do something with the time in between as well, Perfessor."

"Been thinking on that, too. Something to give you a little exercise. Now, I got some friends in Tammany that are always building something somewhere . . ." He paused. "How do you feel about construction, Chopper?"

"I feel fine about it if they give me a living wage. The only thing is . . ."

"What?" he asked.

I felt a little funny about bringing it up, but I had put some effort into studying during the last few months. Given my druthers, I'd just as soon keep working on those brain muscles, too. And there was the rest of my life to consider as well. Nobody boxed forever. I stiffened my resolve and completed my confession.

"Well, the long and short of it is that I started going back to school. High school . . ."

O'Shaunnessey's eyebrows rose once more.

"I wouldn't mind continuing with that. It wouldn't interfere with my nights at all. Not like night school," I added.

Fast. "If I could make just enough on your exhibition bouts to deal with the rent, and maybe pick up a little part-time work on the side—"

The rest of my words were cut off by a yelp and a very ungentlemanly oath emanating from a corner of the gym. The Perfessor and I both spun toward the sound. In the midst of our deep discussion I hadn't noticed the room beginning to fill up with exercisers. Hadn't paid any more attention to the curious machines dotting the rest of the floor at intervals, either. This particular corner machine was the oddest of all. It looked like a horse without its skin, and the club member astride it was bouncing wildly, swearing and hanging on for dear life.

"It's not part of my domain," O'Shaunnessey began, "but I'd best go save the silly bugger. He went and got himself stuck on the mechanical horse." The Perfessor trotted off, muttering, "These new-fangled machines'll be the death of them all yet. Why can't the members just stick with their fists like a civilized person?"

I followed, curious. By the time we arrived, the horse was bucking like a bronco in a Wild West show. O'Shaunnessey reached up to keep the swell from falling to his harm. I ducked below, toward the chugging motor beneath the saddle. It didn't take but a brief moment of study to figure out how to stop it. As the creature hissed and settled into silence, the swell slid off the saddle into O'Shaunnessey's arms.

"Ah, Professor O'Shaunnessey." The gentleman extricated himself, regaining his aplomb. And there was lots of aplomb to be regained, starting from the silver-tipped hair at his temples, the long, patrician nose, and working right on down past the square jaw and well-tended body. "How can I thank you?"

"For starters you could stay off this ridiculous beast. For seconds you could pass the thanks to John Woods, the young man who figured out how to haul in its reins, and is currently fiddling with the innards."

I pulled myself out and up. "It's not a problem, sir. The control was set at top speed. I've lowered it. The motor could do with a bit of grease, though—"

The gentleman was staring at me. "You understand how the contraption works?"

"Of course, sir. It's a simple motor, a—" I almost launched into a description based on lessons learned in my machinery class back at school. He shivered and waved a hand to stop me.

"I'm not interested. I'm only interested in having it function competently in future. Are you capable of arranging that?"

I pulled out a handkerchief from my trousers to rub off the grease on my fingers. "Yes, sir. I could arrange that."

He swept his hand around the huge room in a wide gesture. "The other exercise machines. Can you see that they're working well and safely, too? On a permanent basis?"

What was he asking? Who was this man? I nodded. "Indeed I could, sir."

"Then, Mr. Woods, you are hired." He turned to O'Shaunnessey. "Arrange to have him put on the payroll, Professor. Half-time should be sufficient. But *permanent* half-time. I'll mention the expenditure to the rest of the board. The safety of our members should be our number one priority here at the club."

"Absolutely, sir." O'Shaunnessey was nodding his head in agreement. "Absolutely. I'll get young Woods on the payroll immediately."

I stared at the distinguished back of the distinguished gentleman as he straightened his thin frame and carefully removed himself from the gym. Then I looked at the Perfessor. "Who was he?"

"Only the president. The president of the New York Athletic Club himself." O'Shaunnessey shook his head, then reached up to fondly pat the polished wooden neck of the mechanical horse. "And here I was, set on damning this marvelous beast." He gave it another loving pat, then offered me his best grin. "Instead, it gave Mr. John Aloysius Xavier Woods the opportunity to prove himself to be a mechanic of some parts—"

"But, Perfessor," I protested, "I only pulled out the plug! Any idiot could have—"

"*Sssh.*" He placed a hand on my shoulder. "Just any idiot can't think on his feet—or his knees, either, as the case may be. Being a mechanic of some parts, I think you deserve a living wage, even part-time. How does fifteen dollars a week sound to you, Chopper? To keep the machines in running trim, and maybe do a few other odd jobs about the place? After school, of course."

I sagged against the glorious horse, my head was spinning that fast. Fifteen dollars a week was what a full-time construction worker made. Someone who had paid all his dues to those politicians down at City Hall. When the spinning finally stopped, I raised my eyes from the polished floor I'd been focused on while trying to order my thoughts. "It sounds like heaven, sir."

"Then you accept the employment?"

I nodded, and the spinning began again. "Do I ever!"

"Five afternoons a week, three or four hours the day, whenever you get let out of that school you seem to believe you need. Starting right now. I don't think we dare let this horse throw any more board members."

I squared myself on my feet. "I don't know how I can ever thank you, Perfessor—"

"Nonsense." The grin returned. "You brought it on yourself, boyo. I just hope you really know something about machines."

What I didn't know about machines gave me another reason to return to school. My machinery class teacher was delighted to have me back for the spring semester. He was even more delighted by my sudden spate of questions. But truth to tell, the equipment at the Athletic Club was machinery of the simplest kind. There were bicycles that never went anywhere, and implements to strengthen the arm muscles of the young men who would be rowing crew on the Harlem River come spring. There were terrible, torturous-looking instruments to help a fellow pull heavy weights. But those were mostly all pulleys and levers and just needed constant adjustments. And the balance beams, rings, and trapezes needed nothing but a regular sanding to keep down the splinters.

I bought myself a little toolbox, and slowly filled it with wrenches and pliers and screwdrivers and spouted tins of thick oil. I began studying the quality of the metal and workmanship that went into each tool. I haunted hardware stores, and only bought the best. A good part of my earnings went into that box, and I became inordinately proud of it. I carried it like a doctor toted his satchel, from the tenement all the way uptown to the club each day. And when I arrived, I didn't mind entering the club through the back door—the servants' entrance—either. It was still the New York Athletic Club, the grandest establishment of its kind in the entire world, and I was a part of it.

When I ran out of things to oil or polish in the big gymnasium, when I tired from my daily round of testing each machine, I'd do a few circuits on the running track that edged the upper level of the gym. Next, I began studying the workings of the Turkish bath which the members usually adjourned to after their exertions, or the *natatorium,* which was the club's fancy name for a big long pool for swimming. Everything was interesting. There was so much to learn.

Meanwhile, O'Shaunnessey would tutor one fellow after another in a little paneled boxing room lined with glove-filled racks, or in the gym's center ring. I watched him go through the same process he'd gone through with me for all those months in the Tombs. Over and over again. The man was a born teacher. He was patient, and giving, but he knew the exact moment to stop being patient and put on a little pressure.

My admiration for O'Shaunnessey only grew. And on the best afternoons in the gym, he'd call to me from the ring.

"Chopper!"

"Yes, sir?"

"Barnes could use a little extra workout. Can you spare us a few minutes?"

"Just let me wipe the grease from my hands and get into gloves, Perfessor."

Then I was back in the ring again. Back where I belonged.

★ ELEVEN ★

It took longer than either of us expected for O'Shaunnessey to organize those exhibition bouts. It took longer because he really meant to *organize* them. The Perfessor wasn't satisfied just spending his nights hanging around Brodie's and other saloons on the Lower East Side looking for pugilistic material, although he did do some of that. He also got in touch with other athletic clubs, like one on Long Island, and others as far off as Philadelphia, Cleveland, and even Chicago. His idea was to promote some talent, to have fighters matched by weight, making the competition more equal, and to have two or three separate weight division fights in a single night. And he meant to set up an entire season of these bouts while he was at it.

"You're the one who got me thinking about it, Chopper," he said. "It was one thing putting you up against Skelly in the Tombs, since that was a natural grudge fight—"

"I'll say it was," I threw in.

He grinned. "—and you being so puny, anybody would've been bigger. But it's entirely another thing to have Brodie set you up against those bruisers in his pit night after night. That's not *sporting!*"

"Still beat 'em, didn't I?"

"Now don't get chesty on me. And don't go giving yourself a big head, either, Chopper. We get some properly *trained* competition in your weight division for you, and you beat *them,* then you can change your hat size."

"Yes, sir, Perfessor." It was my turn to grin.

So I'd pull my old cap over my head and strike out for home each night as the winter just sort of battered on. I say battered, because it seemed uncommonly cold, on the outside and on the inside, too—the kind of cold that cudgeled a body like the iron fists of a heavyweight.

Our coal stove being the only source of heat in the flat, we all tended to hang around it as late as we could, nights. Maggie had gone through her Christmas drawing paper so fast I had to lug home a leftover roll of un-inked newsprint I talked the pressmen out of at the *New York World* that I passed each day. Now there was so much paper in the place I had to find some colored chalks so the twins could sit around the table with us and make believe they were doing homework, too. They liked working on letters of the alphabet much better than helping with Ma's forget-me-nots and roses. Ma began to bridle.

"You're trying to make geniuses out of them beforetimes, Johnny, and after I finally taught them how to neatly glue the centers to the stems!"

I glanced up from my Shakespeare. Mrs. Rosen had moved forward from grammar to real *literature*, and *Macbeth* was getting sort of interesting. Those old guys sure and certain knew how to fight dirty. I wasn't sure I would've been willing or able to stand a round in the ring with them. "If that's so, then the twins have learned the lesson and there's not much more to be gained from the exercise. Time for them to move on, Ma. The way Maggie and Bridget and Liam have."

"But they could be helping. It's unproductive, Johnny!"

I set down *Macbeth* with a sigh and picked up a pencil. "I'll show you what's unproductive, Ma." I did a few calculations. "Take these forget-me-nots. You need to make five hundred of 'em to be paid a nickel, right?"

Ma nodded over the mound of forget-me-knot blossoms at her end of the big table.

"And how long does it take you to make those five hundred flowers, Ma?" I asked that as patiently as I could, though I could feel my patience disappearing fast on the subject of artificial flowers.

"When everyone was helping, the way they used to, we could do it in an hour!" She was pleased by that, I could tell.

"That's six man-hours for a nickel," I noted. "And the roses, Ma. What about them?"

"Well, they do take longer, certainly, but I make an entire dollar and twenty cents for twelve gross—"

My pencil was skittering across paper again. "Twelve gross.

eight roses, correct?"

Ma nodded.

"And how long does that take?" I knew, but I pressed her anyhow.

"If it's just me, the way it's been lately, and there are no interruptions—"

"Interruptions such as cooking, or cleaning, or looking after the kids?"

Ma frowned. "About two days. Two twelve-to-fourteen-hour days."

My pencil stopped. The figuring was finished. "Ma, you're making less than a penny a dozen for those roses." I glanced at my sheet again, "In fact, you're making eight-tenths of a cent per dozen. Is it worth it?"

Her fingers stopped their incessant labor. "What do you mean, is it worth it?"

"I mean I'm bringing home enough to get us by. And my job at the club is permanent. You don't have to keep doing this, Ma. Wouldn't you rather be spending your flower-making time—at least part of it—taking the twins for walks when the rest of us are at school? Looking in the shops. Looking at people. Getting some fresh air for all of you?"

"But, Johnny!" Ma's face began to crinkle, as if she were set on breaking into tears. Maybe I'd gone too far, but I didn't stop, even though the little ones were giving me looks like I was suddenly some kind of unspeakable villain. Macbeth himself. "Wouldn't you, Ma?"

Then the tears came, and the sobs. "But it's all I know how

to do! It's, it's the way I can help! Ever since your father disappeared the way he did . . ."

I pushed back my chair, pulled out my handkerchief, and walked around the table to give it to my mother. "I'm sorry, Ma. You *have* been helping." I ignored the snuffles starting on down the table as I rubbed at her neck while she blew her nose.

"You've been wonderful, Johnny," Ma sniffed. "Ever since, ever since you got out of jail . . ." That started off the next round. I rubbed some more. "But you're not here most of the time. I have to feel"—another blow—"*useful.*"

Useful. I changed my tactics right then and there. "You've always been useful, Ma. We couldn't get by without you. But think about something else, Ma. Something else that would make you feel useful besides these everlasting artificial flowers!"

She hiccuped. Maggie dashed to the stove and fetched a cup of coffee. She handed it to Ma and we all watched her sip at it. Finally she set it down, right atop a pile of forget-me-nots. Didn't even seem to notice.

"When I was young, Johnny, before all this . . ." She waved around the tight room. "Before I fell for your father . . ." We all watched a drip of caramel-colored coffee ooze down the side of her cup until it ended, splat, atop a paper blossom. Ma's head jerked. "Back then I used to make all my own clothes. I studied the pictures in the ladies' magazines, and just knew how they'd be put together . . ."

I was kneading Ma's shoulders now, the way I'd seen the masseur at the club work on the swells. "What if you had a sewing machine, Ma?" I asked. "Would you enjoy making clothes again?"

"Oh!" She looked up. "If I had a sewing machine, I could take in piecework. Men's trousers, or shirts. I could make much more than with the flowers!"

My hands dropped from their ministrations and I stormed back around the table to *Macbeth*. She hadn't got the point at all. The point about killing herself over demeaning work. For less than pennies. Would getting out of the tenements make her understand? Or would she just keep on doing piecework in a cottage in Brooklyn, instead of tending a garden, instead of watching the children grow? I growled and slammed into my chair, then growled some more, until Liam prodded me.

"What is it, Liam?"

"It's time to clean out the ashes, Johnny."

I twisted the pencil in my hands until it snapped. Pa hadn't had to deal with all this. He hadn't dealt with any of it. Just changed his address from the local saloon to nowhere. "Then let's clean out the ashes." I scowled at the other kids. "Finish your homework, all of you, so you don't have to spend the rest of your lives making artificial flowers."

Once the evening, Liam shoveled the coal ashes from the stove so I could cart the bucket down the four flights to the ash barrel waiting on the street outside. It was dusty work, making me look more in the way of a West Virginia miner than anything else. And there were other perils attached to the job, too, ever since the end of the whooping cough epidemic.

Wouldn't you just know it, but Maureen O'Reilly took to trotting up and down those same flights it seemed like every blessed time I did. Almost made me think that girl had her ear pressed to the door two flats over from us, just waiting for the slam of my own door, and my own footsteps. Maybe she did. I still couldn't help noticing her cool loveliness—all dark and pale the way she was. But it was her persistence I began noticing more.

"Top of the evening, Johnny!" So cheerful she was with that little lilt to her voice.

"It's past nine, Maureen. I'd call that *night*."

"It's not night at our place till my pa gets back from the saloons."

I rested the heavy weight of the ash bucket on a step and tried to rub the coal smudges from my face. Most likely only added more. It was drafty and so cold that my breath froze right there in the stairwell, but she didn't seem to notice. She was obviously just warming up.

"Then when we hear him coming, we've all got to dive for our mattresses and pretend to be sleeping. Of course, you haven't got a problem like that, with your pa gone and *you* in charge of the family—"

"It's nothing I bless him for, Maureen." I grabbed at the bucket handle again. "Only thing it's taught me is not to be all-fired anxious about setting up my own personal family anytime soon. You'd best get back upstairs, before you catch the pneumonia."

Her face caved in, the way Ma's had when I tried weaning her from those blasted flowers. Then there I was pulling out my spare handkerchief. "Here." I offered it. "You need something else on your mind."

"Something else?" she cried. "What else should be on my mind besides keeping the little ones from killing each other, and keeping our pa from killing us when he gets home drunk? Why can't you be on my mind, Johnny? You work, and you take care of your family, and you don't drink." She swiped at the tears coursing down those china cheeks. "And sometimes you're even kind."

Bang went the bucket again. Then my arms were around her, coal dust and all. What was it about women and tears? "Get yourself away from here, Maureen. Away from the tenement. That's what I'm working toward—"

"Away where, Johnny?" she wailed into my shoulder. "Who'll look after the babies, and where's there to go?"

A picture came into my mind as I gripped her softness to my hard chest. It was of those pretty little waitresses who served the meals at the Athletic Club. Sometimes they were all over the place, showing off their frilly white aprons and starched caps. I eased her head up from my shoulder and caught her eyes with mine. "Let your ma look after the babies, Maureen. They're *her* babies, after all. You're old enough now. Go into service at one of those posh mansions uptown."

"As a maid?" Her wail increased in intensity. "Or a nanny looking after other people's babies?"

"For money, Maureen. For pay. Besides, there's things to

be learned in those mansions. About a different kind of life from here in the tenements—"

She pulled away. "It's so easy for you to say, Johnny. Everything's so easy for you!"

"What?" I yelled. "What's so easy?"

But she'd already stomped off up the stairs. I picked up the bucket and dragged it the rest of the way downstairs and out the door. As I emptied it into the big barrel, a gust of wind blew most of the ashes right back at me. I stood there spluttering in the cold, coughing and rubbing my eyes. Ready to fight anyone stupid enough to get in my way at that particular moment. Even having a permanent job didn't seem to settle anything.

★ TWELVE ★

The next weekday possible I stopped in the bank on my way uptown to work. I withdrew some of my Brooklyn cottage money and tucked it in my pocket. When Saturday came around, I set Maggie in charge of the little ones and dragged Ma out of the flat to go shopping. Shopping for a sewing machine. Even if she wasted it on piecework, it was still a step forward.

Ma settled on a Singer. I put my foot down, though, and not only on the treadle. I insisted on the higher-priced model, the one that came in a small cabinet with drawers. You could drop the sewing head right down inside, close it, and end up with a nice little piece of furniture. It was also the model with this exotic picture painted in gold right across its head. The salesman said it was an Egyptian sphinx and the Pyramids. I was taken by it, and by those golden sand dunes billowing off to either side, too. I figured if Ma was going to be staring at something for hours, it might as well be something interesting. At mass the next day, Ma stood in a pew surrounded by all of us as usual. But I noticed she held her head a little higher than usual. Maybe that was a beginning.

Monday after school there was a new beginning at the gym, too. O'Shaunnessey's welcoming grin was wider than ever as I set down my tool kit and peeled off my coat.

"It's all set, Chopper! At last!"

It took a minute to catch on. All the way uptown on the Sixth Avenue El, I'd been going over things in my mind: sewing machines, and Shakespeare, and women—Lady Macbeth and Ma and Maureen O'Reilly all wrapped up together. "The fights?" I dumbly asked.

"What else!" He jabbed a playful fist right into my belly. Hard. "Friday night is the first set of matches. Then every Friday through the spring. Get through your chores fast, boyo. We've training to begin."

I got through my chores fast. All the little readjustments needed after a weekend of heavy activity at the gym. All the picking up. Why did it seem as if the establishment's entire collection of weighted Indian clubs was scattered over what felt like an acre of polished floor on this of all days? Finally I was ready and the Perfessor set me to a regular program. Two miles of laps around the track, workouts on the striking bags, a few rounds of sparring in the ring. When it was finished he led me into the Turkish bath.

"What now?" I asked.

"Now," he answered, "as the New York Athletic Club's official great hope, you get to use the rest of the facilities. Just like Mr. Roosevelt or Mr. Belmont. Pick a booth for your clothes, Chopper. You've watched the members. Strip down to a towel and we'll take some steam."

"Me?"

"You. After the steam and the plunge, we'll get the masseur to work you over."

"*Me?*" I repeated, just as dumbly as when I'd first arrived at work.

"You," the Perfessor verified. "And we'll be doing the same each and every day. It's the new regimen. The club members have been watching you, Chopper. They like what they see."

"But my job—"

"Your job is secondary till fight season is over. There'll be some heavy bets moving around. The members would prefer winning, and you're their chance to cash in. Potentially."

"Ah," I commented, still numb. At the moment I didn't feel at all like a sure bet. After all that exercise I felt more like a used-up carthorse on his way to the knackers. But I allowed the Perfessor to lead me into the baths.

Surrounded by clouds of steam, O'Shaunnessey turned expansive. He started talking again, the way he used to nights in the Tombs. He expounded on his philosophy of life, and he rehashed memories from his past, but none of it was ever boring. Somehow he always managed to connect his stories to boxing. And with those white puffs of moisture surrounding us, cutting us off from the rest of the club, the rest of the world, I could lie back on the smooth white tiles and let his talk swirl around and through me.

"It's a funny thing about fear, Chopper," he'd start. "Some fighters, they go into the ring with stage fright, the same as actors. What're they afraid of?"

He answered himself without my having to even twitch in his direction.

"Maybe the audience. The rowdy crowds howling for blood. More likely their opponent . . . You go into the ring with that kind of attitude, pretty soon you're scared of getting hit. When you're scared of getting hit, it means you're scared of getting hurt." He paused. "And when you're scared of getting hurt, your days of boxing are numbered."

I contemplated his words behind closed eyes. "You ever feel that way, sir?"

"Me? Never. And I'll tell you why, too."

He rearranged himself to reach for a case and pull out one of his rare cigars. I opened an eye long enough to watch him light it. The smoke disappeared into the mists of hot steam. "Why?" I murmured.

"The Civil War," he stated with complete conviction. "I joined up when I was fourteen, Chopper. Being an orphan, I had no one to hold me back. The enlistment money looked good, too." He puffed. "I marched with Sherman right to the sea. Had friends shot down to either side of me along the way. Coming out of that, I figured a few bruises couldn't ever really hurt me."

"Maybe the Tombs was my Civil War," I thought aloud.

"Could be. Whatever it takes to change a fellow from a boy into a man."

The steam encircled us, a living thing. Past and present merged. Hidden thoughts drifted from me.

"I've never felt fear going into the ring," I confessed. "I feel something different. Not sure how to explain it. Power? Maybe that's it. The power to be in control of one thing in my life. I feel strong. As if that's the very place I was always meant to be . . . And my opponent? It's almost as if he's not a person but an object to be *conquered* . . . Sometimes I think I'd like to be boxing every single day, every single moment. Just me inside the ropes, conquering the world."

O'Shaunnessey laughed. "It's lucky for you, then, that the sport's changing over to Queensberry Rules. In the old London Rules days, when I was fighting barefisted, it took weeks to recover from a bout. The broken knuckles, the gouges. Some fellows even spiked their boots and tried to get at your insteps to lame you. When I was too young to know better, I let a son of a gun take jabs at my eyes. Just little pokes they seemed like. But round after round of little pokes, all in the same spot—my eyes ended up so swollen I had to get my second to lead me to the scratch line for the last rounds. Then I had to hold open an eyelid with my right, and fight one-armed with my left."

"The referee didn't call the fight?" I asked.

The Perfessor snorted. "As long as you could stand up, you fought. But I was completely blinded for three or four days afterward. I even spent that blind time in jail, with the fellow who damaged my eyes in the same cell as me, tending them."

"You weren't angry with him?"

"It was business. How could I be angry? He taught me a useful lesson." O'Shaunnessey chuckled. "The police busted us both, fair and square. And he was the most gentle nurse I've ever had."

What a strange thing this fight business was. What a strange passion. The steam swirled in again.

The masseur took me in hand after O'Shaunnessey and the steam had relaxed me till I felt I hadn't a bone in my body. The masseur didn't talk. He threw me on a table and pounded. Sprinkled liniment oil and pounded some more. Pounded and rubbed and grunted. His grunts had a whole entire range to them, though. By the end of the week I could decipher them as easily as New York English: the questioning grunt when he poked a stretched tendon; the sharp grunt when he wanted me to turn over; the satisfied grunt when he'd nearly finished; the indifferent grunt of dismissal. When I rose from that table I was ready to pull my clothes on again, ready to face whatever the world outside the club had waiting for me. I understood why the sporting gentry fought to be admitted to the New York Athletic Club.

O'Shaunnessey did right by me that entire week. He was a manager any boxer would be willing to fight for to the death. When I finished my regimen on the last night, the night of the bout, he stood waiting for me as I strolled out of the baths in my street clothes, as fit as any fellow had a right to be. As fit as a dozen Vanderbilts.

The Perfessor was holding two things. One was a wrapped parcel, the other was a newspaper. He presented the paper to me, already folded open to a middle page.

"What's this, sir?"

His finger jabbed at a column. "You made the papers, boyo. You made the *National Police Gazette!*"

I walked to the row of columned arches at the side of the gym to hold the paper under the nearest light. " 'Pugilistic News,' " I read aloud. " 'A Close and Accurate Résumé of the Arenic Events of the Week.' " I scanned down the column till my eyes hit on a name I knew. " 'The many admirers of Professor Mike O'Shaunnessey—' You made the papers, too, Perfessor!"

He nodded, as if it happened every day. "Keep reading, Chopper."

I did.

"The many admirers of Professor Mike O'Shaunnessey will be pleased to learn that the popular retired middleweight champion is sponsoring—in conjunction with the New York Athletic Club—a series of weekly exhibition bouts of the highest quality. Tonight's offering has O'Shaunnessey's protégé, featherweight Johnny 'the Chopper' Woods, matched against none other than the protégé of John L. Sullivan, Patsey Kerrigan. We look forward to reporting the outcome."

I stopped. "Featherweight. Seems like I've filled out to the next division." Then the real news registered. "Patsey Kerrigan? John L. Sullivan's protégé? You matched me against *Patsey Kerrigan* tonight? I thought it was just some unknown from a saloon. Like me. You never told me! Why didn't you tell me—"

O'Shaunnessey grinned. "I like to keep a few little surprises tucked up my sleeve, Chopper."

"But, but—"

"But what? You really think you're just some unknown from a saloon? You think you're not ready for Patsey Kerrigan? You're *scared* of him?"

"I'm *not* scared of him," I bristled. "But he's the protégé of John L. Sullivan! The heavyweight champion of the entire world! The Champion of Champions!"

"And *you're* the protégé of Professor Mike O'Shaunnessey." The Perfessor took me by the arm. "Let us withdraw to my private quarters, Chopper, where I'll tell you a little story about my encounters with John L. Sullivan. And also give you this parcel I've been lugging around."

That distracted me. "What is it?" I suspiciously asked.

"Only your official fighting tights, boyo. In club colors."

O'Shaunnessey had hooked me again. I followed him to the boxing room.

★ THIRTEEN ★

Patsey Kerrigan had two or three years on me, an inch or so of height, and eight pounds, according to the Athletic Club's scale. He stood across from me now on the raised ring in the center of the gymnasium, muscles rippling, altogether splendid-looking in tight white knee breeches held up by a multicolored sash. As lightweights, we were the first scheduled bout of the evening.

In my own corner—equally splendid, I hoped, in my club colors of crimson and white—I waited next to O'Shaunnessey for the bell. He was seconding me, which was a right and proper service to perform for one's protégé. John L. Sullivan was most definitely *not* seconding Kerrigan. The Champion of Champions was out of town. Not that anyone had even remotely anticipated his showing up. Not the mob of sports dressed to the nines in top hats and derbies crowding around the ring. Not even me, naïve as I was on the subject. But I wasn't nearly as naïve as I'd been before the Perfessor's private talk with me in his boxing room before ring time.

"I first ran into Sullivan in a Boston saloon, Chopper," he began. "He was massively big, an untried lad of about twenty, in perfect health and stamina—not yet having succumbed to the temptations of drink and wayward women." O'Shaunnessey sighed. "He begged me—I was middleweight champion, remember—he begged me to give him a go in the ring."

"And?" I asked.

The Perfessor handed me the parcel at last. "Squeeze yourself into these tights while we talk, boyo. We'll pass on supper till after the fights. You'll work better on an empty stomach."

"What about Sullivan?" I prodded as I began to remove the shirt I'd barely gotten on my back.

"I did give him a go, but not immediately. Other things came up, like a dislocated shoulder from my scheduled Boston fight." He chuckled. "You'd think I messed up that shoulder on purpose to ruin Sullivan's future, he was that upset with me over it. He had an Irish temper broader than his own shoulders. Still does. But he got over it and set out to make himself a reputation without me . . ."

The bell rang and I pushed John L. Sullivan's story aside to better deal with his protégé. He came at me easy, almost in a glide. No sudden rush, only a thoughtful approach as if he meant to test my caliber. I liked that. It meant he was thinking. It meant he could be a worthy competitor. I was thinking, too, as we closed in. Trying to think of Patsey Kerrigan as an opponent, not as Patsey Kerrigan, protégé of the greatest fighter alive. Trying to find that distance. It was hard separating him from his mentor.

I let him jab first, meaning to measure his strength. It was an easy jab to the chest, like his approach. No force to it. I snapped back with two quick jabs and a right to his own chest, directly under the heart, but my punches had power behind them. He backstepped gracefully, not letting on to the crowd that he'd felt the punches. But I could see he had. I followed through, still easy, wanting to give the sports some action for their money, but also wanting to stretch that action through the four scheduled rounds. Got Kerrigan in a corner and gave him a little more before he spun me away by the elbow and eased himself out. Nice. He knew the moves. Then he tried dancing around to play for time until I cut him off and we were back in the center again. By this time I had Kerrigan's number. He looked good, and he wasn't scared, but he was more interested in looking good than in flat-out fighting. How had *he* come to be chosen as a protégé of the toughest brawler in boxing history?

"By the time I got back to Boston," O'Shaunnessey's tale had continued, "Sullivan was boxing in a ten-cent museum. I was booked into a regular theater for exhibition bouts, and Friday nights I usually closed by taking on a local. So I gave Sullivan his chance, even though he had thirty pounds on me, not to mention his height. I had so much confidence those days, I thought I could take anybody." He chuckled.

"And did you?" I broke in.

"The son of a gun came at me like a windmill, his arms were flailing so. By the third round I was fairly tired. Sullivan wouldn't have anything to do with scientific boxing, wouldn't move around. He still won't. Just stays right there in the center of the ring and strikes out at you like the classic barefisted pugilists. It was me who had to keep moving. So I thought to knock him out and get it over with. I gave him a right hook that should've taken off his head . . ."

"And?" I asked.

"And Sullivan was that tough, instead taking off his head, I broke my hand on it!"

I whistled. "What did you do then?"

"I fought with my left until he stalked off the stage. Just walked out in the middle of the round muttering, 'That will do.' And there I was, with a broken hand wasted on a man of no reputation."

The Perfessor's words echoed back at me. Even the great John L. Sullivan had been a man of no reputation once. I gave Patsey Kerrigan a perfect O'Shaunnessey grin and set about beating down his pretty defense as the bell rang.

"What're you two fellows doing out there?" the Perfessor complained as he wiped me down. "This wasn't meant to be a picnic luncheon."

"Just sizing each other up." I smiled. "I think I've got him figured out. He's real pleased with himself, but the cockiness is all he's picked up from John L. Sullivan."

"Prove it!" O'Shaunnessey barked as the bell rang.

Kerrigan and I moved together faster this time. Patsey started putting on more of a show. And yes, maybe he had picked up something from Sullivan, 'cause there he was, stealing the windmill technique from his mentor. But I'd been forewarned and blocked him till he tired himself out. Then I went in low and hit home in his belly, remembering to retreat fast before he tried Sullivan's other trick.

"You can't lead carelessly for Sullivan's stomach," O'Shaunnessey had declared as I laced up my new canvas ring shoes.

"Why?"

"He chops you on the back of the neck with his right hand. And that right's where all his strength is. He pulled that on me during our second fight in Boston. Thought I'd been hit by a telegraph pole."

So I pulled out fast, missing Kerrigan's telegraph pole. Then I decided to try turning tables. When Patsey came in low at me, I gave him the opening, nice and innocent. Off he went for my belly, and down came my right on the back of his neck. He fell. I stood there several seconds into the count until retreating to a corner. There I waited until Kerrigan struggled up just before the referee yelled "Eight." I shook my head. Thought I'd packed more into that wallop. Either Patsey was tougher than I believed, or I wasn't anywhere close to Sullivan's strength yet. I pushed off the ropes to meet my opponent again.

I never would match Sullivan's strength. It wasn't reasonable. A featherweight wasn't born to be a heavyweight. It was that simple.

"John L. ran about one-eighty-five when we first met up, Chopper," O'Shaunnessey had informed me. "The next time we crossed paths, he'd ballooned to two hundred. But he'd already made saloons his second home by then."

"Drinking?" I asked. "Wouldn't that mess up his training?"

"I'll tell you, boyo, Sullivan wasn't ever the one to let training interfere with his social life. He came to me one day, asking would I go on the road with him for his exhibition tour of the country. This would've been back in '81, just before he won that big match against Ryan in Mississippi. Best decision I ever made, not to join up with him." O'Shaunnessey pulled a pair of gloves from the rack on the wall and weighed them in his palms. "These ought to do for tonight. Let me strap you up a little."

I held out a hand, fingers splayed for the wrapping. "You turned down a chance to tour with Sullivan? It would've been interesting. It would've been—"

"It would've been hauling him out of saloons every blessed night before the show. It would've been helping him into his tights, pushing him toward the curtain, and hoping he wouldn't stagger into his opponent before he mauled him."

"Oh." There'd been that problem with Pa, too, only he hadn't ever managed to make any money out of his drunkenness. "Then how did Sullivan—how does he—keep winning?"

"Brute force. Sheer brute force. But the crowds always loved him. They still do. Why, the man won as much as fourteen thousand dollars in one single bout!"

"*Blue blazes!*" That would buy a lot of real estate.

The Perfessor finished the wrapping and held out the gloves for me to shrug into. Then he glanced at the big clock hanging on the wall over the glove rack. "It's about that time, Chopper."

It was time, all right. Time to forget about Sullivan. Patsey was up from the tight canvas floor, but only barely. He stumbled over his feet and I caught him in my arms. I could've let him fall again, I guess, but I wanted to finish him off properly. By the book. He hugged me almost gratefully while I loosed my right to pound at his side. Then he had his bearings again and stepped back. In the split second before he got his defenses in place, I went for his jaw with my old uppercut. I usually saved that punch, but there didn't seem any reason to stretch things for another two rounds. My right connected and Patsey was down again. This time the count finished, all the way to ten.

The bell rang as the referee held up his hands signaling the end of the bout. Even then I hardly believed I'd knocked Kerrigan out. Knocked out John L. Sullivan's protégé. I hadn't ever intended to knock out Patsey Kerrigan—certainly not in the second round. He'd just made it all too easy. He hadn't been the opponent I'd expected.

Only then did I notice the stunned growl of the crowd change into cheers. Only then did I notice O'Shaunnessey by my side.

"What in the name of heaven were you up to tonight, Chopper?"

"You didn't like the results?" The Perfessor was raising my arm in victory. I nodded to the crowd. "That last uppercut was all mine. As for the rest, I was just testing some of those John L. Sullivan techniques you told me about."

O'Shaunnessey dropped the arm to swat my behind. "Remind me not to tell you any more stories, Chopper."

The Perfessor took me to a chop house for a late supper after the fights were over. We brushed cigar smoke from our path to settle at a table surrounded by the bustle of serving waiters and the raised pints and voices of the sporting crowd. Waiting for our rare steaks to arrive, I pulled out my purse for the evening. It wasn't exactly what I'd anticipated. But it was beautiful. I snapped open the pocket watch to inspect the timepiece inside.

"That's an Elgin, Chopper," O'Shaunnessey said. "The

best. The case was designed by a club member. And it isn't just plated. No sir, that's gold pure through and through."

I closed the watch to admire the club logo—the winged foot of Mercury—etched on the front, then turned the whole thing over to read the inscription on the back:

NEW YORK ATHLETIC CLUB
EXHIBITION BOXING CHAMP
SPRING, 1886

I sighed. It wasn't going to buy me a cottage in Brooklyn. "I guess I needed a watch," I said.

"Every gentleman needs a watch," O'Shaunnessey answered. He slipped something across the table to me. "But every boxer needs money. The club has to keep its amateur status, so it can't be giving proper purses, but a few of the members enjoyed your two rounds enough to pass on a little tip."

I took the offering and glanced at it under the table before pocketing it. Fifty dollars. I smiled. "Will they enjoy me more if I go four rounds next time?"

"Chopper! For shame! Monetary considerations should never make you forget the sacred nature of the sport!" But the Perfessor was still grinning as the steaks arrived.

★ FOURTEEN ★

The purse for the second bout I won at the New York Athletic Club was a solid gold medallion—suitably engraved—meant to be a matching fob for my club watch. After the third bout I received a solid gold chain to hold the whole works together, watch and fob both. The tips remained the same.

I spent a certain amount of time—mostly during Shop Mathematics at school—considering what percentage of a cottage the entire ensemble would pay for. I even thought in passing about maybe consulting with a pawnbroker on the subject. In the end, I couldn't do it. The watch and its attachments were too handsome. I'd never owned anything so fine. And I'd earned it all fair and square.

Meanwhile, the expenses at home just kept rising. With the coming of spring, every blessed one of my brothers and sisters sprouted like they were flowers. Maybe I'd been feeding them too well. As I had no intentions of altering that situation, they were all going to need new shoes and clothing. But it wasn't until after those first few bouts that I snapped out of whatever haze I'd been in and began noticing those changes.

The first was the flat itself. One day I woke up and noticed I wasn't tripping over the remains of artificial flowers anymore. They were all gone. All except for one lavish bouquet still sitting atop the table in Pa's old beer growler. Ma's new Singer sewing machine now held pride of place directly beneath the light from the lone window. On Sundays it was closed up neat as you could please and the growler vase was moved to the center of its polished wooden top. The rest of the week it lay wide open, surrounded by new piles: piles of men's trousers Ma was doing piecework finishing on.

Ma was changing, too. The sewing seemed to suit her. She didn't work as long into the night, since she could now make twice the earnings in fewer hours. That didn't mean she stopped sewing come darkness, though. Instead, nights while the rest of us worked on our studies around the table, there was Ma peddling up a storm on the foot treadle. But nighttime was for her. Nights she fussed with outfits for the girls and herself. And she hummed, or let up on both humming and stitching to make conversation while she was doing it.

"I met Mrs. O'Reilly while the twins and I were out picking up more trousers today, Johnny."

"Yes?" I hauled my attention from the history book I was reading. It was talking about the economic benefits of the digging of the Erie Canal some sixty years back. Didn't say anything about the proper construction methods, though.

That would have been interesting. Didn't say anything about the sweat of all the Irishmen who had built it, either.

"I told her about your gold watch—"

"Ma! You didn't!"

"I told her about the medal, too. And why not? I'm not allowed to brag a little about my son who's supporting us all?"

Why not was that Mrs. O'Reilly would head directly home and pass on the gossip to Maureen. And before you knew it, Maureen would be stalking me through the hallways again. Tempted as I was, I still didn't have time for any romantic nonsense. That girl had an eye for the breadwinner, and she definitely wanted out of the tenement. Almost as badly as me. I didn't like the idea of being anyone else's meal ticket. My family was enough. "It's private business, Ma. And besides, those fights at the club aren't bringing in nearly as much money as I'd hoped."

"Thirty dollars a week is still a grand amount of money, Johnny."

Thirty dollars is what I'd told Ma. The other twenty went straight into my secret account at the bank. It wasn't a lot, but slowly the balance was building. "It's hardly grand," I objected. "Not when you figure on new shoes for the family, and clothes for Liam and Jamie, since you only make girls' stuff." I tried to find my place in the book again, then gave up for the moment. "And not when you also figure on those little extra odds and ends, things like another lamp so you don't go blind nights at the sewing machine . . ." I glanced over to her. She was bent too close to the cloth. "Will you be needing spectacles, Ma?"

Her head jerked back guiltily.

"Certainly not!"

Slowly her head crept closer again. I added the price of an eye doctor and glasses to my list and continued on with my itemization. "Then there's the cost of using Mr. Chin's laundry regularly—"

"I told you that's an unneeded expense, Johnny!"

"What, you liked it better when we had ropes strung all over the two rooms and there was always laundry dripping on everything?"

"Not during the spring and summer it wasn't. There's the roof for that on nice days—"

"Not to mention puddles all over the floor from the washtub, and your hands always red and chapped nearly raw from the lye soap. You liked that, too, Ma?"

Ma sighed. "Well . . ."

I wanted to get back to my work, but I knew Ma needed to talk, too. She didn't see nearly enough people. I eased up on her. "So we'll let Mr. Chin keep fighting with the steam and the lye. What else did Mrs. O'Reilly have to say?"

Ma brightened. "You'll never guess! Her oldest, Maureen?"

I nodded as nonchalantly as I could.

"She's gone and got herself a position in one of those uptown mansions. On Fifth Avenue! As a maid. Can you imagine!"

"Oh." That was why Maureen hadn't been around the halls. I thought maybe after our last meeting she was still angry with me. Instead, she'd gone and taken my advice. "So."

"She has Thursdays off and comes home to visit then."

"Thursdays. That's nice." Nice to know. I'd be especially careful on Thursdays.

Ma turned back to her machine, satisfied for the moment. I began sketching in the margin of my history book. Sketches of what I thought a working canal lock would look like.

School was going fairly well for me again. The machinery class had begun a new session on drafting and blueprint reading. We students got to tear apart the milling machine that sat squat in the center of the workshop's cement floor. Next, we learned how to draw the parts very precisely on paper, like a toolmaker. Then, of course, we had to put everything back together again. It was a good way to learn how machines were made, how they worked, and I enjoyed it above all my classes.

I enjoyed learning how to use a compass and T-square and mechanical pencil, too. The precision of the drawings pleased me. I'd never considered myself the least artistic—not like Maggie. My fingers couldn't come up with a pretty picture if you'd offered me a million dollars. But my fingers—even with my thickened knuckles—seemed surprisingly able to come up with millimeter-sized changes to that milling machine. Alterations for threading patterns so minute, they'd need to be measured by a caliper. One day my teacher noticed.

"Ever consider becoming an engineer, John?"

I straightened up from the drawing board. "What, sir?"

"You've a natural aptitude. Like Edison."

"Thomas Edison? The genius?"

He laughed. "You're not a genius yet, John. But you've potential. See that you sign up for science next year. And more math. Real math, like algebra."

Next year. I hadn't got that far in my planning yet. "And after that?" I asked. "What do I do after that to become an engineer?"

"Well, first you complete your high school diploma. Then you apply to college for another four or five years of study—"

I groaned. Here I'd been thinking that if I could only manage to get that one piece of paper, that high school diploma, doors would begin opening for me.

Mr. Sparkman smiled. "Nothing in life comes without a little effort, John. But if you've the will, you can make it." My teeth ground together as he patted me on the shoulder. "Think about it. Not everyone has been granted the potential."

So there was another thing for me to think about. And meanwhile, something else came home from school beside my jumbled thoughts. And it came home with Liam.

"Bugs!" Ma screeched one night while she was readying the little ones for bed. "You've got *bugs* in your hair, Liam!"

The girls made a mad dash for the bedroom and Liam set in to crying while I slammed shut my textbook. "What next?" I muttered to myself. I went over to the washstand to investigate the situation. "It's only head lice, Ma. Itchy, but nowhere near deadly. Most of the prisoners had them in the Tombs. In Bummers' Hall, *everyone* did."

Ma was wringing her hands. "But this isn't jail, Johnny. I try so hard to keep a clean home—"

I gave Ma a hug. "It's got nothing to do with you or your cleaning habits, Ma. They're fine." I bent down to Liam, who'd moved on to a howl. "It's all right, fellow. You brought them home from someone at school. We'll just need to wash your hair before the teachers notice and decide to shave it all off." I ignored the howl's increase in decibels to look up at Ma. "With lye soap. That's what they used in the Tombs."

That helped pull Ma together. "Maggie!" she ordered. "Stop hiding in the bedroom and get out the washtub. Right now." She turned to me. "It's late, but I'm afraid you'll have to haul some water up from the courtyard pump. We've only what's on the stove."

"Not a problem, Ma. And Liam can help, since he's the culprit."

So there we were, Liam and I, hauling water up four flights of stairs past nine o'clock of the evening. I added something to the specifications and the price for that little cottage in Brooklyn: running water. While I was at it, I added something else I'd recently learned about, but not at the Tombs. Something I'd learned about at the New York Athletic Club: an indoor privy. An indoor privy complete with one of Mr. Thomas Crapper's finest ceramic water closets. Since I was going for the moon, I threw in a bathtub, too. One of those bathtubs with the little feet that looked like a lion's paws—

"Your face is all scrunched up, Johnny." Liam stopped to rest his sloshing, half-filled bucket. "What are you thinking about?"

"Creatures, Liam."

"Like the creatures living on my head?" His fear had already changed to fascination.

"Those, and other creatures, too. Ones from far-off places like Africa, in the Central Park Zoo."

"The zoo! Will you take me there one Saturday, Johnny? I'd give up baseball at the park—at least for a week—to see a zoo!"

I groaned, but not too loudly. "Sure, Liam. We'll go to the zoo. But we'd better take Katie and Jamie along, too. Maybe even Bridget and Maggie. The whole lot of us could pack some food and have a picnic there. Maybe even Ma."

He thought about losing his special private time. After careful consideration, he made up his mind about it. "That would be all right. But only for a picnic and the zoo."

"Only for a picnic and the zoo," I agreed.

We continued up the stairs.

By the end of O'Shaunnessey's scheduled program of fights I'd also picked up a silver cigar case and a match safe monogrammed with the same winged foot. I hadn't any immediate intentions of taking up with cigars, but the match safe was useful. The final purse was closer to the real thing. It was a reddish-brown, prime leather wallet hand-tooled with the familiar symbol. When I checked inside the billfold, I found that my tip had doubled for the night. The last night. I glanced across the usual chop house table where the Perfessor and I were celebrating my final win with the usual rare steak.

"What happens next?"

O'Shaunnessey cut into his inch-thick sirloin and carefully chewed and swallowed a hunk. "Well, Chopper, the season is over at the club, and I can honestly say I'm going to miss it. However"—he set to with his steak again—"however, your name has been cropping up in the newspaper columns with satisfying regularity the past few weeks."

"So?" You see your name in the paper once, it's exciting. After that, the novelty wears thin. There's always another name to push yours off the pages of *Leslie's* and the *Police Gazette*.

"*So?* That's all you can say?" He grinned. "At least celebrity doesn't seem to go to your head like some nobs."

"Celebrity doesn't pay the rent. Not all by itself."

The Perfessor nodded. "Truer words were never spoken. You've got a brain in that head, boyo, as well as two strong fists."

I only shrugged. O'Shaunnessey noticed.

"Eat your steak. It's getting cold. You'll need the strength for what's coming up."

The forkful of meat halfway to my mouth stopped in midair. "What's coming up? What haven't you told me now?"

"I don't like to be too precipitous, Chopper. Never have. I like to have my bird firmly bagged before I start the cooking fire."

The fork clattered onto my plate. "I can't stand it, sir! What are you planning?"

"As I started to say . . ." He made a careful show of eating another quarter of his meat. And it was a huge quarter. Finally he let up. "Richard Fox—"

"Richard *K.* Fox of the *Police Gazette*? The owner and editor himself?"

"The same. Richard Fox apparently has had his eye on you. He prefers heavyweights—been in a feud with John L. Sullivan for ages now, trying to bring down the big boy's title—but he also enjoys lightweights. As do I," O'Shaunnessey professed. "They've got more agility, put on a better show in the ring—"

My patience had its limits. "I know all that, Perfessor. I'm a lightweight, remember?"

"Only too well." He whipped his napkin past his mustache and the grin emerged again. "To put it in a nutshell, Fox contacted me the other day. Wanted to know if I'd be willing to put up half of a deposit, if he put up the other half—"

"On *what*?" My voice rose, then broke. I tried again, lowering it with effort. "A deposit on what?"

"A deposit prior to signing articles of intent for a professional bout. A *prizefight*. For you, Chopper. As the opener for a middleweight fight."

"When?" I asked.

"This summer. Probably July."

"Where?"

"That is a thorny problem. We can't pull this one off as an exhibition bout right here in the city. There'll be the police to worry about." He glanced at his remaining meat, then pushed the plate away. "We might have to do it out of the country.

Maybe take a few boats up to Canada. A number of fights have come off successfully on this little spit of land called Long Point, not too far across the water from Buffalo."

"What's the purse?" I slung some meat in my mouth.

"For your bout, two thousand."

Nearly gagged. "After your cut, which you've never properly gotten yet, and expenses, that would leave me—"

"A thousand, Chopper. A cool thousand."

My fork clattered onto the plate. "When do we start training?"

"Well, here it is the end of April already, Chopper. And you're in prime condition. Why don't we just *stay* in training?"

"You mean the same regimen each day at the club? The members won't mind?"

"The members will be filling those steamboats to Canada, boyo."

"Maybe I'd better finish my steak, then."

O'Shaunnessey pulled his plate back toward him. "Maybe I'd better finish mine, too. We're both going to need our strength."

★ FIFTEEN ★

After that, the spring went fast. Between classes, and my job, and the training, and Saturdays spent with the kids, and Sundays at church, there was barely time to think straight. Barely time to finish my final drafting designs and study for exams. There surely wasn't any time to worry about July.

Yet I found the time. Mostly in the middle of the night it was, with me wedged next to the kitchen table in my blankets—or up on the roof under the stars as the weather warmed. Who would Richard Fox and O'Shaunnessey match me against? That was the big question. It certainly wouldn't be one of the amateurs O'Shaunnessey had hauled in from Long Island and even Chicago after I'd bested Patsey Kerrigan. I'd even berated the Perfessor on that score.

"What amateurs?" he complained in a rare show of temper. "I matched you with the best up-and-comers I could find, Chopper. Is it my fault you sometimes turn into a machine in the ring? All cogs and wheels grinding. You're almost relentless." He stopped. "You blaming me because you won?"

"No, sir," I sighed. "That last match, Jed Brown? He did give me a little competition," I allowed. Grizzly Brown was my first black opponent. He came into the ring with chest and arms oiled to mahogany magnificence. Made me feel like a ghost next to him. When a few of his punches hit home, though, I knew I wasn't any ghost—just up against someone who was maybe trying his hardest at finding a way out of the tenements, same as me.

But this July fight, I knew it would be different. Down in my gut I knew. My opponent would be a professional—a different kind of professional than I'd met so far, no matter what O'Shaunnessey claimed. Someone who'd been fighting hard. And winning hard. Someone who'd worked his way up the tough way, like me. I began paying closer attention to the *Police Gazette*'s listings of completed and upcoming fights. Trying to get a handle on who my competition would be, and what kind of a record—and reputation—he had, little knowing that I'd be getting some tougher competition sooner than I'd expected.

It happened the week after school was finished. O'Shaunnessey had wrangled me a raise to twenty dollars a week, knowing I'd been missing those "tips" from the fights. Now that I had more time, I spent a good piece of it at the club, trying my best to really earn the money, to give value where it was due. So there I was, swinging my tool kit and climbing the four flights of stairs after a long day of work and training, trying to figure if it was Thursday or not and I'd have to be on the lookout for Maureen O'Reilly. Finding myself slightly disappointed when she didn't pop out of the woodwork. Wondering if maybe I ought to stroll by that Fifth Avenue mansion she was working at, just to see what kind of a place it was. Couldn't hurt. I'd be doing it on my terms, and it might be a sociable sort of gesture. She might even want to go for a walk in Central Park. I nodded to myself. As soon as I got past the big fight. Pleased with my decision, I got to the door, swung it open, and froze.

"*Pa!*"

There he was, big as life, sprawled like a king in Ma's usual seat at the head of the table. Older than I'd remembered Pa was, his thick red hair gone to gray, his body gone to paunch. Spread out around him was the rest of the family, the little ones with their supper plates untouched, looking terrified; Ma hovering by the stove, looking . . .

"As I live and breathe, my son and heir. Johnny." Pa pushed back his empty plate and smirked. "Or should I be calling you *Chopper*?"

My tool kit thudded to the floor. Waves of anger washed over me. My stomach cramped up. My entire body went feverish. And none of it came from the summer heat in those tight rooms. Still stunned, I watched as the tableau changed slightly around me. Ma picked up the coffeepot, seeming unsure whether to pour the liquid into a cup or atop Pa's head.

"He's called *Johnny* at home, Jack."

"What are you doing here?" Finally found my voice again, and it came out in a bark. "*Why* are you here?"

"What kind of a welcome home is that for a man come all the way from Boston?" Pa growled.

"The kind of welcome you deserve after abandoning all of us over three years past!" I shot back.

Pa got to his feet and tried to sling an arm around Ma. She shrugged him off. "I missed my wife and children. Is that a crime?" He made another attempt at Ma, a rough kiss. This time she slapped him.

Ma standing up for herself like that—it was a wonder. It was also my signal. I waited for Pa to consider even raising a finger against my mother. He thought about it, I could see it in his eyes. Instead, he backed off, and I made a show of closing the door to the hallway while I took a few deep breaths. The stomach calmed a little, but the fever was still with me. I turned again to the room, to my father.

"Why now, Pa?" Why now, when we'd finally worked him out of our lives. Why now, when we were beginning to make a go of things on our own?

Pa squared his shoulders, trying for that old cocky look. "I can't come home to congratulate my famous son?" He strutted around the table and gave me the same arm he'd thrown around Ma. "A chip off the old block if I ever saw one."

I didn't shrug him off, though I wanted to more than anything. Just stood firm. Like a rock. Unfortunately, the fever had gone to my brain and my voice wasn't nearly as steady as I'd hoped. "Never call me that! I'm not like you! I never want to be, and never will be!"

His arm dropped, then his fingers rose to pluck at the chain dangling from the vest I wore over my shirtsleeves. With a flick, he pulled out the watch. "Quite the gentleman you've become. Complete with gold watch and chain." He found the medallion. "Gold fob, too. How can a gentleman be saying such things? To his own father, who begat him!"

I pulled the dangling watch from his hands and tucked it safely back in its vest pocket. "That's all you ever did for me, Pa. All you ever did for any of your children."

His face hardened. I could see the red rising to purple in the veins that disfigured his cheeks and nose. His fists balled up, then loosened to pull at his belt. "I've a mind to take the strap to you, boy. Like in the old days."

O'Shaunnessey's discipline took over long enough to let me regain control of my emotions. "You'll never be taking your belt to me again, Pa. Nor to any of the others. Not in this lifetime."

"Johnny!" Ma begged from across the room.

I glanced at my mother. "Do you want him back, Ma? After what he did to you all those years? After what he did to all of us?" I paused. "After what he *didn't* do these past three years?"

Before Ma could answer, Pa bellowed out, "What makes you the new head of this family, Mr. John Aloysius Xavier Woods?"

I stared him down. "I stayed, Pa. You left."

"Well, now I've returned, and you'll all have to get used to the fact all over again. You, especially, *Chopper*." He spat out my nickname like it was a dirty word. All at once I knew why he'd come home.

"You read about me in the papers, didn't you, Pa. You read about the big fight coming up. You're not back out of duty. Surely not out of love. You're back to cash in on my wins."

"You young bastard!" His fists bunched up again.

"Wrong word, Pa. I'm the chip off the old block, remember? What would that make you?"

His right struck out for me. But I was ready for it. More ready for what was coming than Pa realized. I ducked. Then my right came up. My power punch. My uppercut. It only took one shot—straight to Pa's jaw. Calm now at last, I watched the blow connect. Watched Pa's head jerk away. Watched the little dance his feet did as his body swayed. Watched him tilt backwards to strike his head against the edge of Ma's sewing machine. Watched him crash to the floor. Then I stood there, feeling nothing but the throb of my bare knuckles.

"Johnny! Oh, Johnny!" Ma cried. "What have you done to your father?"

"I knocked him out, Ma. Fair and square."

Ma stood poised between the dry sink and Pa's body, tears running down her cheeks. At last she methodically reached for a towel, dipped it in water, wrung it out, then rounded the table to bend over Pa. "Take the little ones for a walk around the block, Johnny, while I deal with this. Make it a long walk."

I suddenly remembered the rest of the family. There'd not been a peep out of a one of them during the entire affair. They still all sat numb as statues—pale and wide-eyed statues—but Maggie and Bridget were beginning to tremble.

"Are you sure, Ma? Will you be all right?"

"Yes. Your father and I need to talk."

"Sure thing, Ma. Good idea."

I made it a very long walk. All the way to Broadway and the nearest ice cream parlor. I stuffed all of them with ice cream to make up for the supper they'd missed, then back on the street topped it off with bottles of ginger ale from a street cart. Twilight was falling before we passed the corner candy store by our building. I ran the kids through that, too.

Outside the tenement steps, Liam burped, almost spitting out his jawbreaker. He made a fast save, then asked, "Is Pa gonna be coming back like this often, Johnny?"

"Why?"

"It'd almost be worth it for the ice cream."

"And ginger ale," Jamie piped up.

"And candy," Katie added.

It was Maggie who turned on the little ones before I had the chance. "No. He's not! And you should be ashamed of yourselves for asking such a thing!"

"No more ice cream?" Liam asked.

I ran swollen fingers through his hair. "There'll be other times for ice cream. For better reasons."

"Then it's all right," Liam declared. "Was that an uppercut you gave Pa, Johnny? It was a whopper! Will you teach me how to do it same as you?"

Pa was gone when we got back to the flat. Ma wordlessly sent all the kids straight to bed. Then she poured us both a cup of coffee and we sat together at the table.

"I'm not sorry for what I did, Ma," I started.

She waved a hand wearily. "He brought it on himself."

"Is he gone, then? For good?"

"He's gone, but who knows for how long, Johnny?" She reached for my arm. "He found your silver cigar box before he left. I'm afraid it's gone, too."

I shrugged. "Cigars are bad for a boxer's wind anyhow." Then I remembered something. "He didn't find your house-keeping money, did he? Your private stash?"

Ma gave me a weak smile. "That's one blessing. And it wasn't for want of trying. The man was in such a rage when he came to his senses that he tore into all the mattresses searching for it."

"But he didn't think to look under the artificial flowers in his old beer growler, did he?" I grinned.

"No, he didn't." Ma laughed; then her laughter turned to sobs. "Johnny, what are we going to do next? What can we do?"

"You truly don't ever want him back, Ma?"

She shook her head. "He wasn't a bad man in the beginning, Johnny. He did try to support us all. But everything—a new baby always coming, the terrible jobs, the tenement it-self—it just wore him down. Tore him apart. And there were the saloons waiting. Half a dozen on every block." She sniffed back another sob. "After a few drinks he felt like a man again. After a few more . . . I can't have him back. Not ever. I know I promised to love and obey before God Himself, and *I* could stand the torture, but I'll no longer be putting up with it for my children. Not God and all His saints could make me do that anymore."

"God wouldn't want you to, Ma."

I watched my mother stiffen her shoulders, watched her head rise, almost as high as she held it in church. "I've moved somewhere beyond Jack Woods."

"That's progress, Ma." I fetched a clean handkerchief from my pocket and passed it over. Watched her mop up the damage. I hadn't wanted to mention my plans before—my plans for Brooklyn—but if ever the moment was right, this was it.

"Let me tell you how we're going to make even more progress. How we're going to move so far beyond Pa that he'll never find us again."

★ SIXTEEN ★

I'd stopped Ma's tears, sure enough. But in the doing—in the sharing of my secret plans at last—I'd also made it inconceivable to lose the big fight coming up. Ma had real hope in her eyes for the first time since I could remember. How could I take that away again by failing?

Sure, I had a decent chance. I was undefeated. But a boxer only stays undefeated until he meets his match—or better. Sooner or later everyone falls. I just didn't want it to be during this fight. I prayed it wouldn't happen this fight.

Make my fists like steel, Lord. Turn my body to stone. Let me win.

It ran through my mind like a litany. I wrestled over the subject with each and every one of my saints, too. I wasn't taking any chances. Ma wasn't, either. Her new rosary was getting plenty of exercise as she pleaded with the Blessed Mother for me.

And all this time she never said another word about Brooklyn. The calendar hanging over the sink said it for her. It was becoming tattered from marking off every day that passed between my bout with Pa and the circled July fight date. Each big X was a small victory, a respite from Pa. The closing gap was the purgatory she had to survive in fear and trembling. Would Pa turn up again? We knew he would. He'd be hiding out in some saloon, building up his bluff for a return engagement. Would it be before my big fight, or after? Would we make our escape from the tenement in time?

It wasn't only praying I was doing, either. I trained twice as hard, twice as long, until even O'Shaunnessey noticed.

"You figure you're going up against Sullivan himself, Chopper?"

"If that's who you've matched me against, then I want to be ready."

He punched me just under the ribs. My skin didn't even twitch.

"Look at that." He rubbed his knuckles. "Like stone. You're becoming obsessed, Chopper. You need a rest."

"No! I have to be ready, I have to—"

The Perfessor took hold of me by the shoulders and shook. "You are ready, boyo. Any more ready and you'll destroy yourself. You've got to have something else on your mind besides this fight."

"I've got plenty else on my mind!"

O'Shaunnessey stopped the shaking to eye me. "You think

I don't know that? You think I don't see the way you drag in here from home every day? It takes you three miles on the track just to get the haunted look off your face."

I dropped my eyes and said nothing.

"There you go, fighting your own wars in private, like usual. You don't have to tell me the details, Chopper. I don't need 'em. But you do need to remember that I'm on your side. I'm your biggest fan. And I aim to get you loosened up before this fight. Before you go out there and kill your opponent."

My head bobbed up. "How? How will you do that?" It was almost a challenge.

"Well now, I'll have to spend some time thinking on the problem. In the meanwhile, why don't you go and take apart the innards of that mechanical horse again. It seems to relax you."

"Yes, sir." I fetched my tool kit and headed for the horse, even though I already knew its innards by heart. It did relax me.

"Niagara Falls!"

Four days before the big fight, and that's what O'Shaunnessey greets me with.

"Niagara Falls?" I dropped my tool kit in a corner of the boxing room and began stripping for my run.

"The solution, Chopper." O'Shaunnessey's grin nearly broke his face in half. He pulled some tickets from his pocket.

"I just came from the train station. You and me are going to do some touristing before the big fight. We're heading up tomorrow, before the rest of the touts. I've booked us straight through on the excursion line from Buffalo to Niagara Falls."

I stared at the Perfessor as if he were out of his mind. Maybe he was. "We're going *sightseeing* the day before my biggest fight?"

His grin remained undiminished in intensity. "We are. It's just what the doctor ordered. Dr. Michael O'Shaunnessey. Run through your paces fast, then get on home and pack a bag, boyo. I'll meet you here at the club at seven in the morning."

"But, but—"

"We shall gaze, and tremble as we gaze, just like the posters say, Chopper. We'll also have ourselves a few thrills unknown to the ring."

"But—" I was beginning to sound like a stuttering fool. "But—"

O'Shaunnessey gave me a solid thwack on the back. "Less said about the rest the better. It's time we both had a little fun for ourselves. It's time we *played*."

I finished changing and took my frustrations onto the track. Play? What was that? I ground my feet harder into the run, punished my body worse than usual.

The Perfessor and I and our assorted paraphernalia made it onto the train on time the next morning. We stowed our bags and settled in. I got the window seat. It was wasted on me. Twenty minutes out of New York City for the first time in my life; twenty minutes on a real train—not the el—for the first time in my life, and I was asleep.

I must have slept for hours. When I woke, O'Shaunnessey was peacefully sucking on a cigar, his eyes focused on the window beyond my slumped body. I shifted a shoulder and glanced out.

"Mountains?" I'd never seen mountains before.

"Part of the Appalachian chain," O'Shaunnessey replied, as if we'd been holding a continuous conversation all these hours. "I like a nice mountain or two. Even enjoy hills in a pinch."

I rubbed my eyes. "You let me sleep."

"You needed it."

I gave him silence for an affirmative, then, "When do we arrive?"

"This evening. I booked us rooms in a hotel on the very rim of the falls."

"Good."

I stared out at the gentle curves of the tree-covered mountains. Never seen so much green before, either. But the *clickety-clack* of the train's wheels on the tracks was hypnotizing. My eyes closed again. They stayed closed for the rest of the journey.

O'Shaunnessey jostled me awake long enough to help transfer our gear to the hotel. I staggered through the lobby like the living dead, seeing nothing. In my room, I crashed onto the bed and slept some more. All the way till morning.

"These are the best bacon and eggs I've ever tasted!"

O'Shaunnessey shoved over a platter stacked high with pancakes, then another filled with pork chops. "Top 'em off with a few of these, Chopper."

With the food the grogginess was passing at last. I focused on a pork chop long enough to ask the obvious question. "Should I be stuffing myself today? With the big fight tomorrow?"

"We'll walk breakfast off this morning, and take it easy on the other meals. Go ahead, Chopper. Enjoy."

I did. Finally sated, I pushed back my chair. "Where are those falls, Perfessor?"

"You've been staring at them out the dining room window for the past half hour, boyo. No food or drink . . ." He shook his head. "Nothing but sleep for a solid twenty-four hours. That always make you blind, Chopper?"

I jumped up, suddenly raring to go. "Can't say, Perfessor. I never tried it before."

He threw down his napkin and trotted after me.

Then I was standing practically atop the Niagara Falls. I took a deep breath of the mist-filled air. It was like the Turkish baths, only cool, and a million times more—with rainbows.

Rainbows everywhere you looked. And a wonderful roaring that almost made you want to slide over the top and down those falls. Float on and on with the sheer power of the waters. I turned to O'Shaunnessey beside me. "I'm trembling, Perfessor, just like the posters say."

"Good. Then we've accomplished the sublime part of our mission." He grabbed my arm.

"Wait! What're you doing?"

He grinned. "Hauling you off for the fun part. The *Maid of the Mist* sets off for the falls themselves every hour on the hour. I want to catch an early boat in case the experience needs repeating."

The Perfessor wasn't joking. Not a bit. We made the trip on the little steamer to the very foot of the American Falls twice, covered from head to foot in oilskins. We still came back drenched to the bone from the wind-swept spray dashed onto us as we neared close—terrifyingly close—to the base of the falls themselves.

I watched O'Shaunnessey cling to the railing, roaring with all his might into the tempest, as if his roars were challenging the currents, challenging the mighty falls to try to suck the little ship and us into certain death. When he won the dare, when the boat pulled safely away, O'Shaunnessey released his grip from the railing and gave me a playful punch. I punched back. Soon we were sparring on the slippery deck, amazed passengers scurrying from our path. We didn't bother speaking. There weren't any words that needed to be said. Everything just felt right. How small Pa's threat seemed in the light of all the awesome magnificence surrounding us. How small the tenement. I slipped and danced closer to O'Shaunnessey and caught him in a bear hug. He punched out of it. And then there we were clutching the railing again, both grinning like idiots.

Next we stood in line to climb down into the Cave of the Winds. At the bottom, with the daylight, we found ourselves hanging on to ropes strung tighter than a boxing ring, hanging on for dear life as we clambered over a narrow boardwalk past boulders near the very base of the falls.

Then it was time for lunch, and time to wander through all the shops and diversions cluttering up narrow streets around the edges of Niagara Falls. I stood mouth agape watching a fellow swallow fire, right there in the middle of the street! Others were juggling balls, or playing rambunctious music on banjos and tambourines. The Perfessor left a coin in each of their waiting hats. "Got to support professionals, Chopper," he said each time. "We all need to eat."

As for me, I supported the shopkeepers. I bought a pretty blue-and-white plate with the falls painted in the center for Ma. For the kids I purchased a huge box of Niagara Falls taffy. When we ran out of streets and shops, and had even paid the toll to walk over a narrow bridge to Goat Island and admire the sheer drop between American Falls to one side and Horseshoe Falls to the other, O'Shaunnessey turned to me. His eyes twinkled.

"There just might be time for one more go on the *Maid of the Mist* before catching our train, Chopper. How about it?"

I laughed, feeling absolutely prime. "Lead the way, Perfessor. I'm game."

★ SEVENTEEN ★

Our steamboat left Buffalo at midnight to cross Lake Erie for Long Point, Canada. I stood on deck to watch us pull away from the dock, then wandered past toughs and touts, gentlemen and thieves, all littering the decks with their drinks and cigars. Wandered through the saloons filled with gamblers settling into their games for the night. I wandered past everyone down to my cabin, where I tumbled into a bunk and slept again. I didn't worry about the morning fight. I didn't dream about my opponent. I just slept solidly until the Perfessor shook me.

"Up and at 'em, Chopper. Land's in sight. Time for the wake-up exercises—"

"—of your own personal devising," I finished for him with a smile. I leaped out of bed and right down to the floor. Sunlight splashed through the cabin window. As I pumped my body up and down, it felt good to be alive. I was glad. I finished the first fifty and looked up. "Thank you, Dr. O'Shaunnessey. For everything."

He gave me a mock frown. "Another fifty, boyo. Don't try slacking off on me the very morning of the big fight."

I laughed and finished the exercises.

The Perfessor and I leaned into the railing on deck watching Long Point grow nearer. It was nothing but a long spit of sand seemingly in the middle of nowhere, with a wooden lighthouse standing tall to one end of it. O'Shaunnessey pulled at his mustache as he surveyed the scene.

"As you already know, I've been here before, Chopper, for a few other fights. There are sandbars close to the shore, so we'll all have to use small boats for disembarking." He nodded toward the second steamboat that had been shadowing ours and was now slowing to a stop as it closed in to land. "They've already started. Probably the crew who's meant to pitch the ring."

My eyes worked their way from the lighthouse over the entire terrain, straight back to the unbroken line of forest behind. "At least we won't have to worry about police stopping the fight. There's not another soul around, except maybe the lighthouse keeper." I shoved my hands in my pockets. The morning was cool for midsummer. The temperature would be comfortable for an outdoor bout. "So, Perfessor. You going to tell me about my opponent at last? Or am I going to have to meet him blind? All I know is his name, Sam Matthews. That's all the *Police Gazette* and the posters had to say."

"Then you know nearly as much as I do, Chopper. Believe it or not, this one I wasn't trying to keep from you. It wouldn't have made sense." He ran a hand over his bald crown. "I just didn't have enough information. No records of wins or losses. No rumors about his style. Fox was keeping it close to the vest for some reason. It might be part of his betting scheme."

"Hoping for a surprise upset by Matthews?" I asked.

"Could be, Chopper, since the odds are currently in your favor. At this point, all I know is that Sam Matthews is aboard the other ship, his moniker is 'Blinker,' and he's come all the way from Australia."

"From Australia? Not just for this fight!"

O'Shaunnessey smiled. "No, not from halfway around the world just to meet you. But he did come all the way from San Francisco. The purse was tempting enough for that. There's a bunch of Australian fighters turning up these days, trying to make their names in the States. A tough bunch, from what I hear."

I whistled. "They'd have to be to bother coming all that way!"

There was a sudden change in the motion of the ship beneath my feet. The Perfessor felt it, too.

"Look sharp, boyo, I think it's time to head for the small boats." He paused another moment to study me. "I have the feeling you'll not be wanting for competition this bout, Chopper. I have the feeling you'll be working for your purse."

All the arrangements had been made at last. The ships were empty and the spit of land full. The ring was staked right into the sand of Long Point itself. I stood in my corner of it, hardly seeing the several thousand expectant men surrounding me. Barely noticing the score of ringkeepers on duty just outside the ropes to keep order. I was too busy feeling the unusual buoyancy of hard sand under my shoes, blessing the Perfessor for the sand he'd had hauled into the gym for me to spar in over the past few weeks. Like he said, he'd been to Long Point before, and he wasn't about to let the strangeness trip me up. O'Shaunnessey might not know my opponent's record, but he'd done everything else in his power to prepare me for this moment.

The master of ceremonies, Billy Madden, was announcing the day's referee. It was none other than Jack "Nonpareil" Dempsey, the current middleweight champ. The crowd gathered closer around the ring to welcome Dempsey with their hurrahs. They were getting into the spirit, ready for a good time. Then it was our turn, Sam Matthews and I, facing off from opposing corners. Madden gave me the nod first. I felt a little shiver slide down my back as he raised his arms for attention. The mob settled down and let Madden start in on his spiel.

"Now, I know all you patrons of the manly art are excited

about our opener. You've been waiting to see the young pugilist the papers have been talking about. You've been looking forward to watching a future champion—and not too far in the future, either—a future lightweight champion at work!"

The little shiver froze midway down my spine. Me? A future champion?

"Raise your gloves, Chopper!" O'Shaunnessey barked. "Give 'em a show!"

I raised my gloves as ordered. Tried to look good and chesty as Madden finished the intro. And why shouldn't I? My body was in better shape than it'd ever been. Steel and stone.

"Gentlemen, I give you—direct from New York City—the one, the only, the *un-de-feated* Johnny *'the Chopper'* Woods!"

Hearty cheers filled the crisp air. I scuffed the sand with a little dance and waved my gloves some more before retreating back to my corner.

"How's that, Perfessor?" I asked.

"Fine, Chopper. Just fine." But his attention was focused on the far side of the ring. Focused on Blinker Matthews. Madden was already halfway through Matthews's introduction.

". . . all the way from Down Under, via San Francisco, I give you the lightweight champion of Australia, Sam 'the Blinker' Matthews!"

Matthews bounced from his corner like one of the kangaroos I'd seen with the kids at the zoo. He was at least twenty, blond and lean, and his muscles looked like something chiseled from marble. Like Apollo at the Metropolitan Museum of Art. I swallowed. *Lightweight champion of Australia. He was already a champion.* Then I remembered my prayer again, my fists and my body. Steel could smash marble.

". . . going six rounds, Queensberry Rules, for a purse of *two thou-sand* dollars! Gentlemen, let the fight commence!"

The timekeeper rang the gong and the tough Australian and I met at the center scratch line to slap gloves. The fight commenced.

Didn't take long to figure out how Matthews had gotten his nickname. He had a tic in his right eye. Almost like the Morse code it was, signaling his moves. But it could work both ways, that signal. Get hypnotized by it, and you were caught. I fell for it. Once. Took two rough punches to the belly for my sins. After that, I hunkered down to concentrate even harder, but on Blinker's hands, not his tic. Blocked out all the crowd sounds, made my own little world with only two people in it. Me and Blinker Matthews. Me and Blinker fighting like some duel out of Shakespeare. We were only into the second minute of the first round and I already knew it was that serious. Knew that my gut had been sending me true messages all the past month. Matthews hadn't bothered with any preliminary getting-to-know-you's. He'd come at me fighting hard from the gong. I fought back.

When the bell rang, I made it to my corner and slumped onto the waiting stool to heave while the Perfessor fussed over me.

"How'd you get those scratches near your eyes, Chopper?"

"What scratches?" Water from the dipper splashed into my mouth. I spit, then allowed myself a small sip.

"You didn't feel them?" He rubbed me down as I shook my head.

"Listen," he continued in a rush of words. "Protect your head. Your eyes. He's trying to lace you."

"*Lace* me?"

"With the laces on the wrist of his gloves. They can slash deep, cause enough blood to blind you. He's fighting dirty, boyo, and it'll only get worse—"

The gong sounded and I was back in the center again.

So Matthews was dirty. I'd have to back off a little, be more wary. But the more cautious I was, the wilder he turned. He surged toward me like a steam engine. I was watching his hands. There it came. The jab headed for my eye. I saw how he did it. A little flick of the wrist at the last instant, so you got smashed with the inside of his wrist—smashed by his laces—instead of a clean knuckle punch. It took a moment too long to register the information. I spun my head, but he still caught me. This time I felt the scratch, but it was to my ear. Better than my eye. In a moment he went for my eyes, and I was ready with a quick jab to his wrist. It would've broken a lesser man's. Blinker just did a little shrug and made a quick sidestep around me. He'd caught the message. There was to be no more lacing in Round Two.

"Good job, Chopper," O'Shaunnessey crowed as he doused my head with water and rubbed some alcohol on the ear. "He's ahead on points, but you'll catch up. He's not likely to try the lacing again since you caught on."

"There'll be something else, Perfessor."

I waltzed into Round Three with my confidence regained. But I kept my eye on those hands nonetheless. Should've been watching his feet. Not more than thirty seconds into the round, one of them struck out and caught my ankle. I fell to my knees on the sand.

"Foul!" yelled the referee, pulling Matthews off my body.

I rose without a count, spitting mad. He'd really clobbered that ankle. Nearly lamed me. I put the pain to the back of my mind and stoked up my own steam engine. Real speed was out with the injury, but I could still limp resolutely forward. And I did, the soft give of the sand now on my side as it cushioned the excruciating spasms. I went at him like the pistons of one of my machines, hammering into a body I now knew to be granite, not marble. Marble was too soft. I backed him into a corner and pounded. Matthews acted as if he didn't feel a thing, just managed to lift a protecting glove and poke its thumb in my eye.

"*Blast!*" I backed off, letting him escape. Then I had to make a complete circle in search of him—with my left eye closed. Closed because he hadn't merely poked it. There'd been something on that glove, something that burned my eye like fire. Not Skelly's turpentine, either. It was sneakier than that. I got through the rest of the third round by hopping out of rhythm on my good foot, always just a breath from Blinker's fists.

"Chopper!" O'Shaunnessey had caught every move this time. He had a wet rag ready to slap on my eye, then a bandage to strap around my ankle. "You're only halfway through.

You want me to call the fight? This bastard's worse than I thought. He's not trying to kill you fair and square. He's trying to *maim* you!"

"No!" I yelped as the bandage tightened painfully. "No. I'll make it. I'll find a way!"

I would find a way. I limped back to the center of the ring at the bell. Had to find a way. Sam "Blinker" Matthews was not going to rob me of my dreams. He wasn't going to steal that cottage from Ma and the kids. Blinker was nothing but a thief, no better than Skelly. A dirty thief without honor. I'd take him, even half-blind and lame. I'd take him, and I'd do it the right way—the way O'Shaunnessey had taught me.

Blinker came at me laughing. "Had enough yet, Yank?" He was sure of himself. So sure of himself that he showed his teeth. The full set. I plowed an overhand right into them. He spun away gagging. Wouldn't be a full set of teeth anymore.

Rather than pausing to admire my handiwork, I shuffled through the sand and caught him with his head turned to spit out the blood and broken shards. Gave him a left hook to the unprotected side of his head. It connected good and solid, but Blinker must really have been made of granite. He snapped right back with a hook aimed for the side of my own head. My bad eye muddled my vision so that I had trouble seeing the punch coming. I turned my head, and it caught me square on the nose.

Fireworks. Even through the bad eye I could see fireworks. Amazing how pain sharpened the senses. As it washed through me, so did the mob's frenzied bellows of approval.

Bloodlust. They were loving every dirty trick, every vicious blow. They were getting their money's worth.

I ducked, searching for a moment to recover, but Blinker didn't want me to have that moment. He hulked above me, relentless. That's when I noticed that my duck had put me under his defenses, and suddenly my head cleared and something clicked. From my position, Sam "Blinker" Matthews was unprotected! I shot back up between his arms with a roar of anger—and my power punch. The punch that'd knocked out Skelly. The punch that'd finished Patsey Kerrigan. The punch that'd taken Pa. My uppercut to the jaw.

It didn't let me down. Blinker let out a whistled sigh through the new gap between his teeth and sank to the sand. I staggered to the nearest neutral corner as Dempsey bent over him for the count. The long count. All the way to ten. I had plenty of time to concentrate on the numbers. It was better than thinking about the racking pains running up my leg from the bad ankle. It was better than watching the blood flow like Niagara from my nose all over my chest and white tights.

Then Dempsey was dragging me from my corner to the center of the ring. He held up my gloved right hand. Had to. I didn't have the strength left to do it for myself.

"And the winner of this amazing bout," he yelled above the crowd gone mad, "after a fourth-round knockout—the winner is the still-undefeated *Chop-per Woods!*"

O'Shaunnessey swept into the ring to congratulate me.

"I did it," I whispered. "I won."

After which I collapsed into his arms.

★ EIGHTEEN ★

It was resin Matthews had jammed in my eye along with his thumb. O'Shaunnessey figured that out on the way back to Buffalo as I sprawled on our cabin's lower bunk. Neither of us had stuck around for the main event, the middleweight bout. Instead, the Perfessor manhandled me onto a small boat, impressed a few sailors to do the rowing, and got me back aboard the steamboat. Where he proceeded to fuss over me as if he were Ma. Slabs of raw steak lay across my eyes, cold compresses on my nose and ankle.

"Enough," I finally growled, near to suffocating. I lifted the meat and tried to open an eye to stare him down, but found both were useless. "What happened to the good eye?" I asked.

"The swelling comes with the broken nose, Chopper. You're going to have impressive shiners in a day or two."

I winced. "Just in time for my homecoming." Then, "Did you get the purse? You did get the purse!"

"Never fear." I heard him pat a pocket. "Twenty century notes, right here for safekeeping."

"Thank goodness," I sighed. "Then it was all worth it."

"That remains to be seen. Try to get some sleep, boyo. We'll get you to a doctor in Buffalo."

"What war did you come from?"

Those were the doctor's first words as O'Shaunnessey supported me into his office. When we left, I had a patch on one eye, bandages across my nose, a plaster cast on my broken ankle, and a pair of crutches. I didn't even bother to count the stitches the doctor made with a fine needle on various other parts of my body. It wasn't worth it. I had a thousand dollars in my pocket. That's what counted.

I got the window seat again on the train back to New York. I still didn't catch much more of the scenery than I did the first time around. My one good eye hardly opened above a slit. Besides, it was night.

So I sat there thinking about what I was returning to. Questions ran through my mind. Questions about my future. After this bout with Matthews I was beginning to have doubts about proceeding with an extended career as a boxer. It wasn't the pain he'd inflicted. I could live with the pain. That was part of the game. It wasn't that he'd turned me scared, either. But it had been my first truly professional fight, and I hadn't liked the trappings that came with it. The crowd's approval of the fouls. The referee turning a blind eye to most of Blinker's dirty tricks. The sheer savagery of the thing. Most of all, my turning savage with it. My Long Point bout hadn't had any of the beauty of the sport that O'Shaunnessey had instilled in me.

Where did the feeling of control disappear to? My upper-cut had still worked, but I'd used it out of necessity, from a position of weakness, not of strength. The power I once felt in the ring had vanished. I turned my head to the window with a wince. I had time before I made any final decisions on the boxing. It would be months before I was in any kind of shape to even consider another fight. I tried to make out some of those mountain shapes. Instead of my catching a mountain, another question formed in my mind. Maybe it was inevitable.

"Have they got high schools in Brooklyn, Perfessor?" I asked.

In the morning, O'Shaunnessey settled me and my bag in a hack waiting right in front of the train station. I returned to the Lower East Side in style. I hadn't quite got a handle on the crutches yet, so I tipped one of the boys playing in front of my building to haul the bag up behind me. Finally I was there, in front of the door, satchel by my feet. I pushed the door open, afraid of what might be waiting.

Not Pa. I gave a sigh of relief. Only the rest of them, Ma and the little ones, just finishing off their breakfast. Every blessed head turned in my direction. Instead of the eruption of excitement I'd expected, there was silence. It went on too long.

"Isn't anyone going to welcome me home? Isn't anyone going to ask if I won?"

"Johnny. Mother of God, Johnny," Ma finally whispered. "How could you be winning looking like that?"

"You should have seen the other fellow!" I grinned.

Then the kids came at me. I had to stave them off with my crutches until I'd managed to reach into my pocket. Leaning into one crutch, I unfolded my purse money and fanned the bills for the entire family to see.

"Leave the dishes, Ma. Drop everything. Get your shoes on, kids. We're taking a little trip to Brooklyn!"

"And how will you be managing that, Johnny?" Ma asked.

"Believe me, Ma, after what I've been through, getting to Brooklyn will be a picnic."